The facts surrounding the mysterious stranger granting Christmas wishes...

1) No one's *ever* seen him.

2) Money is *no* object.

3) He's taken a *very* personal interest in one particular gift recipient—Sharon Fontaine.

4) He plans to get Sharon a husband—even if he has to volunteer for the job!

Who is this St. Nick—and, more importantly, what does he *want for Christmas?*

Dear Reader,

If Santa told you that the man of your dreams would be waiting under the tree this year, *who* would you unwrap on Christmas morning? A secret crush? Your husband? Tommy Lee Jones? If you'll send me a postcard with a brief (20 words max.) description of your answer, signed with your first name and your city and state, you just might see it printed with others on a special page in the months to come.

This holiday season, though, Santa's busy searching for the man of Sharon's dreams in Hayley Gardner's novel, *Holiday Husband*. The single Scrooge has challenged St. Nick to deliver Mr. Right by December 25. And on Christmas Eve something tall, dark and handsome is coming down the chimney.

But Anne, in Laurie Paige's *Christmas Kisses for a Dollar*, has to avoid meeting the man of her dreams—or else. She'll only date the dullest men her tiny Texas town has to offer. The worse a man kisses, the better! And rancher Jon Sinclair, who doesn't like *or elses*, kisses a little too well....

I hope you enjoy these two holiday treats. Next month, look for two Yours Truly titles by Janice Kaiser and Christie Ridgway—two new novels about unexpectedly meeting, dating...and marrying Mr. Right.

Happy Holidays!

Melissa Senate
Editor

Please address questions and book requests to:
Silhouette Reader Service
U.S.: 3010 Walden Ave., P.O. Box 1325, Buffalo, NY 14269
Canadian: P.O. Box 609, Fort Erie, Ont. L2A 5X3

HAYLEY GARDNER

Holiday Husband

All the Best!
Hayley Gardner

SILHOUETTE | YOURS TRULY™

Published by Silhouette Books
America's Publisher of Contemporary Romance

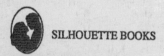 SILHOUETTE BOOKS

ISBN 0-373-52010-7

HOLIDAY HUSBAND

Copyright © 1995 by Florence Moyer

About the author

I have always loved underdogs, the people who have to struggle to obtain their dreams, whether it be a team predicted to lose in a game or a person who starts at the bottom and, through her own spirit and perseverance, quietly comes out on top. Or the girl who stands against the wall at school dances, wishing that the man of every girl's dreams would come through the door and spirit her off right in front of all her more "popular" peers.

I have always loved hearing about the people around us who quietly come through and amaze us with their caring, their bravery or their love for people they don't even know. You hear about them all the time. Throughout the country they appear in droves to search for a missing child, or step into a dangerous situation to help a stranger, or start recreational programs for handicapped children who otherwise would miss out.

These are the people I like to write about; people who want their hearts' desires very badly, but have to put up the fight of their lives to get it, and people who step forward to help when they don't have to and have nothing to gain by doing so. The ones whose stories bring tears to your eyes and gladness to your heart and who deserve happy endings. Like Sharon and Nick in *Holiday Husband*.

Holiday Husband is Hayley's first novel for Silhouette.

This book is dedicated to my own Christmas
Angel, Matthew, and always, to Dan...

And to Faye H., Ms. Scott, Linda D., Donnalee and
Shannon: this book is for you and all like you who
care when you don't have to and who live the
Christmas spirit all year long. And a special
thanks to Betty Loredo.

1

——▸ ◂——

The *Wheaton Tribune*—November 27

You'd Better Watch Out
by Sharon Fontaine

For those of you who haven't heard, for the past two years a mystery man has been extending invitations to some folks in our Missouri town to a "Christmas Extravaganza," during which he gives away a fortune in presents to three needy people he personally selects. Known as Saint Nick, this Santa Claus remains in hiding while he gives people their hearts' desires every year. Well, he's back again this Christmas, and folks, I'll admit it, I'm skeptical.

I know a lot of you are caught up in the spirit of Christmas and the goodness of mankind, but before you call me Scrooge, ask yourself this question: why would someone give his money away? You'd either have to be a real saint, or—my guess—after something. The fact that Wheaton's Santa Claus might be a real saint is too ridiculous to ponder in the reality of the nineties.

Nobody is that good anymore. Which leads me to believe Saint Nick stands to gain *big* at the expense of the people of Wheaton. My personal theory is that Nick is really a businessman, and that this is a publicity stunt—you know, the old "you have to spend money to make a fortune" idea.

Anyway, whatever Saint Nick's doing, he's not stepping forward to talk about the young woman who wound up missing after being one of his gift recipients at last year's Extravaganza. What was *her* wish? Tracy Rhodes's father is wishing he knew. Why doesn't Saint Nick come forward and tell him? Perhaps help him find his daughter?

So, Saint Nick, I'm challenging you to tell us what's motivating you. Come out of hiding, if you dare. And to the good citizens of Wheaton, I'm giving you fair warning—"You'd better watch out." Nothing is ever free. There's always a price to pay for your heart's desire.

Reporter Sharon Fontaine finished rereading the guest editorial she'd written two days earlier and put the paper down on her desk. Already, according to her city editor, Harley Gibson, the paper had received more than a hundred angry phone calls and letters chastising her for her negativity. Harley was beaming at the prospect of increased circulation, but Sharon was disappointed. Oh, not because of the feedback, but rather because the article hadn't done its job. Saint Nick had yet to come out of hiding.

Nearby, someone was humming "We Wish You a Merry Christmas," and Sharon pushed her shoulder-length, dark brown hair behind her ears to insert a pair of earplugs she kept handy during Christmas. She hated the season. It conjured up old memories and the hurt that, with too many Christmas songs, could turn into agonizing pain.

Purposely she turned her thoughts back to Saint Nick. Positive the man had ulterior motives to his generosity, her goal was to expose him, to show the public he was, in reality, no saint. At the very least, she was convinced he was mixed up in Tracy Rhodes's disappearance. Mentally, she reviewed one more time what she knew about the situation.

Fact: Tracy had turned up missing two weeks after Saint Nick's party. Her wealthy father had blitzed the media, but the only lead the police had was that Tracy's boyfriend had left town about a month after she'd disappeared. They'd told Samuel Rhodes that Tracy was of an age to leave if she wanted to be with a man, and there wasn't much they could do about it. The private detective hired by Rhodes had claimed it was as if Santa Claus himself had spirited Tracy off in his sleigh. Her trail wasn't just dead—it was nonexistent.

Fact: A dozen or so people from Saint Nick's party last year had gone to the police in answer to their request for information about Tracy's disappearance. All claimed nothing out of the ordinary had happened at the Extravaganza. They also said that Tracy had not publicly stated her wish, but a man dressed as Santa Claus had announced that Saint Nick would be giving Tracy the present she had chosen. Since the young woman had come home that night safe and sound, the police had not further investigated Saint Nick or the hotel where the party was always held. But Sharon had. The hotel's official statement had been that a Mr. Peabody had showed up to pay them and direct the party and he'd paid in cash.

Fact: Samuel Rhodes, Tracy's father, had claimed his daughter had been depressed before the party, but afterward had been, quote, "On cloud nine."

Now, Sharon wanted Saint Nick's interview.

"Fontaine!" she heard faintly through her earplugs.

Pulled from her thoughts, Sharon grimaced. Her editor was the only one at the *Tribune* who shouted. She pulled out one of her earplugs. "Silver Bells" was playing softly on someone's radio, and she mentally shut the sound out of her head while she glanced around the newsroom.

She spotted Harley leaning down to speak to one of the other reporters. While she waited for him to get to her, she stared around the *Wheaton Tribune*'s busy office. All the reporters were men save for her and Nancy Mantooth, but they were treated equally. They were all working late again to meet tonight's deadline of the almost-medium-size daily they slaved over.

That's what she'd been—one indistinguishable slave out of many—until just recently when she'd come up with the idea of challenging the city's beloved Saint Nick through a guest editorial. Now she was a star, a special reporter, the one with a "cutting edge." Her editor now knew she existed, as did the city, too, if you counted the furious response.

She *had* to follow through, she thought, watching Harley walking toward her again, or be the laughing-stock of Wheaton. The callers and letters to the editor *were* calling her a Scrooge—and worse. She would *have* to find something amiss in Saint Nick's generosity, or no one would ever take her seriously as a reporter again. Her career was all she had to fulfill her life. She couldn't lose it.

"Here, Fontaine," Harley said, tossing a cream-colored envelope with her name engraved on the front onto her desk.

Picking it up, she grinned ear to ear at the underweight, red-haired city editor at her side who had brought it to her. "My Christmas bonus, Harley?"

"Nope, and I'm not giving out early Valentines, either. Just open it, would you please?"

As always, she obeyed. "'Dear Ms. Fontaine,'" she read out loud. "'You are cordially invited to attend a Christmas Extravaganza at the Hotel Sanborn, Ballroom 2A, on December 2, to begin at seven-thirty.'" Her words were slightly muffled in her ears, and she reached up to yank out the other earplug before reading further. "'Please be advised that you are also one of this year's gift recipients.'" Her green eyes narrowed. Just what was Saint Nick up to?

"Go on," Harley said.

"'Ask Santa for whatever you want—money is no object.' Dress—'formal.' It's signed 'Saint Nick'—in ink."

"That's it?" Harley asked, reaching for the invitation. "No RSVP?"

Shaking her head, she handed it to him. "Who would turn him down, Harley? Anything you want, no questions asked." Her resolve to get the story behind the story strengthened. The man had to have something up his sleeve.

Harley's gaze met hers. "What will you ask for?"

"I don't have a clue." She bit back a smirk as she considered asking Saint Nick to buy this newspaper for her so she could be Harley's boss and give him the same hell he gave Nancy and her. Wouldn't that be a scream? But there were sure to be some sort of reporter's ethics for whatever she might ask for, and she'd only have to give it back.

"Don't worry, Harley, I'm going to get what I want. Whether he knows it or not, this Saint Nick is going to have one very busy Christmas this year." She wouldn't rest until she sought out the man behind the mystery and got the scoop on Tracy Rhodes. "I'm going to find out what makes Saint Nick tick."

Harley's face stiffened into his city editor look as he handed the invitation back to her. "Just remember this isn't your only beat. I still need town hall covered and—"

"I won't forget," she told him. "How did you come across this?" She flapped the envelope.

"Somebody slid it under my door when I was out. Maybe that somebody didn't want you asking questions when they delivered it?" His red eyebrows quirked upward.

"Maybe. The plot thickens," Sharon said ominously. "As if it wasn't already thick enough."

As Harley nodded sharply and left the newsroom, Sharon leaned back in her chair, ignoring the rising volume of chatter among the other reporters. She didn't mind being the lone wolf going against Saint Nick, she thought, staring down at her invitation. The public had gone wild over the thought that the mystery man might appear out of the air, snatch them up, and give them their heart's desire. She owed it to her readers to redirect them back to the lottery and scratch-off tickets—which afforded them more of a chance to get what they wanted than Christmas wishes. Unanswered, those only led to heartbreak.

She knew this for a fact. The newsroom faded away as she remembered. She'd been just eleven years old, on the playground at school, telling two of her classmates she'd asked Santa's helper at the department store to ask the real Santa to make her mother well for Christmas. The girls had laughed and taunted her, and with the cruelty of children, told her that her mother was bound to die of the cancer that had made her a semi-invalid if she counted on Santa Claus to cure her. So Sharon had gone home and tearfully asked her mother, one more time, if Santa existed.

Giving Sharon the Christmas angel she'd made for the top of the tree, her mother had told her she should tell the angel her heart's desire and then wish very, very hard, with all her heart, for what she wanted. Then she needed to place the angel on the top of the tree, so it could watch over her. The spirit of Christmas was in every angel and every star on every Christmas tree, her mother had promised, and if Sharon believed in the spirit enough, whatever she'd wanted would be granted.

Late that night when her mother had gone to sleep, Sharon had crept to the tree and prayed to the angel to make her mother well, rubbing her fingertips over its skirt, which was as shiny white as new fallen snow. The angel had rustled with unspoken promise as Sharon had put it atop the small tree, and she had gone to bed with a warm glowing feeling that all would be well.

Three weeks later her mother had died, and she had ceased to believe in Christmas.

The phone on Sharon's desk rang, jarring her from her memory. Rubbing a single tear from her eye and taking a deep breath to ease the pain in her heart, she picked it up.

"Sharon Fontaine."

"This is Catherine," a female said on the other end of the line, quite unnecessarily. Sharon would know her mentor's voice anywhere. She'd met Catherine on a field trip her high school journalism class had taken to the *Tribune*. When Sharon had expressed an interest in working at a newspaper, Catherine Hughes, an experienced reporter in her early thirties, had taken her under her wing, gotten her summer jobs as a gofer, and finally nurtured her right into her present reporter position, where her interest had turned into a gentle obsession to be as good a reporter as her mentor. Saint Nick's story was Sharon's first big chance to meet her goal and make Catherine proud of her.

"Hi," she said, letting Catherine's soft voice wash away some of her pain. "Did you get my letter?" Knowing Catherine would be interested, she'd sent her a copy of her article on Saint Nick.

"Today. That's why I called. I loved your editorial. Has the mystery man gotten back to you yet?"

"As a matter of fact..." She explained quickly about the invitation.

Catherine chuckled. "What are you going to ask for?"

"I'm not certain. Something he can't possibly give me. I have a point to prove. Got any ideas?"

"Not a one," she replied, laughing. "Unless you ask for the man of your dreams."

Sharon blinked. "Money can't buy that."

"Exactly," Catherine agreed. "But aren't you interested in seeing how this Saint Nick would handle your request? It would be quite a measure of his worth, don't you think?"

"Hmm." Intrigued, Sharon scratched the idea down to give it some thought.

"You really can't come for Christmas?" Catherine asked, voicing the real reason behind her call. It was an old argument between them. The one holiday Catherine loved and wanted to share with her, Sharon ran from as hard as she could.

"Sorry, I'm tied up here," Sharon said, knowing full well Catherine would see through her lie. Before her friend could revive their old argument, Sharon asked, "How are the babies?"

Three years before, at age forty, Catherine had abruptly quit the paper after a whirlwind courtship to marry and move to St. Louis, her husband's hometown. Two babies later, she was quite happy being a full-time mom.

"Growing like tumbleweeds." Catherine rattled cheerfully on about her girls, but Sharon only half listened. Oh, she was happy for her friend, but deep in her heart, she envied her. Love was just another wish of hers that seemed destined never to be fulfilled. One broken romance a few years before, and the scattered, "going nowhere" dates since had proven that to her. She didn't even want to try love anymore. It hurt too badly when things fell apart. No, for her, it would have to be her career that kept her happy. Unless...

Unless she followed Catherine's suggestion and asked Saint Nick for a man, and Saint Nick really did answer Christmas dreams, a sort of angel on a treetop. Could it be possible? Dare she believe again?

"Let me know how this Extravaganza goes," Catherine said.

"I'll write you all about it," Sharon promised, her mind skimming the possible ways Saint Nick could find her someone to love. Want ads, hiring an escort, personal friends, she couldn't imagine he'd find someone she could really love through any of those means. She could show him up as the threat he was to people's happiness....

Or she could end up happy herself.

"Sharon?" Catherine prodded.

"Hmm?"

"Merry Christmas."

No matter how heartfelt, Catherine's wish to her felt like a handful of snow down Sharon's back, cooling the excitement she'd felt over the possibilities at the Extravaganza. Who did she think she was kidding? Christmas wishes never came true. She knew that.

"Yeah," Sharon said and then sighed. "I'll keep in touch." She added a goodbye, hung up the phone, and stared at the invitation on her desk.

Was it her imagination, or did it yet again seem to whisper a promise? Could this saint, this paragon, find her love? Or was she falling into the same trap the people of Wheaton were?

She was almost afraid to find out.

Friday night, invitation in hand, Sharon stood square in the doorway of the Christmas Extravaganza, listening to the band play the elegant dance music. Uh-oh. She'd blown it already. The men all wore black suits, the women, long gowns of velvets or sequins in festive Christmas reds, greens, silvers and golds. In comparison to the other guests, she felt like somebody's poor relation in her white silk minidress and flashy red purse. It was her own fault—the invitation had said formal. She'd just thought with Santa Claus showing up, people would have been a little more relaxed.

Well, she was here, and too fashionably late to go home now and change. Nothing to do but make the best of things.

"Excuuuse me," said a nasal, masculine voice behind her.

An apology on her lips for blocking the way, Sharon whirled around on the toe of one glossy white pump. The strangest man, with slicked-down hair so wet it looked black, stood glowering down at her.

She caught her breath. Hiding her surprise and a giggle, she bowed her head and slipped her invitation back into her purse. Except for the sexy scent of Scotsman Cologne that lingered around him, he was every person's version of a classic nerd. He wore a red-and-green striped tie and a clashing yellow plaid suit that sagged on him, even though he was tolerably tall. Too tall for the suit, as a matter of fact, since his socks were showing to his ankle bones.

"Nice socks," she said.

"They match the tie," he said, his tone quite serious.

She got it now—he was the evening's entertainment. A comedian, comic...whatever they called themselves nowadays. "So who's your tailor?" she asked brightly. "I admire people who start new fashion trends."

He stared down at her with an intensity that made her shut her lips tightly together. Through glasses so thick she could see the layers of the lens reflected in the dim light of the room, she read dislike in his narrowed eyes.

"You're not a comedian?" she asked.

He shook his head. "Excuuuse me. I am needed elsewhere."

She stepped aside. If those glasses were real, the man had to be almost blind, which might explain his clashing clothing, and then again, it might not. Watching, she saw two of the guests gape as he proceeded down the aisle toward the long table in the back that held a huge punch bowl, various foods, and an assortment of lovely china. Every so often, his hand darted out to touch the wall, almost as if he was using it to guide his way.

He didn't look like he belonged here, and it was possible he'd gotten the wrong party, misread the banquet hall name on the door or something. After her faux pas upon meeting him, the least she could do would be to apologize and point out his mistake before someone else did and embarrassed him. Frowning, she hurried after the man, reaching him just as he bumped into the table.

"Uh, sir," she called.

He stopped, stiffened, turned, and looked down at her again. She tried to meet his gaze, but looking through the thick lenses made her feel seasick. "I'm sorry about annoying you before. But, were you aware this is the Christmas Extravaganza? I thought you might have gotten the wrong room, what with your eyesight problem and all."

"I don't have an eyesight problem. No, I don't," he said. His shrill, nasal voice split through the waltz music, and heads turned toward them. He snorted loudly, obnoxiously. "You must have an eyesight problem though, since you couldn't read the invitation. It specified formal. You are semiformal. Yes, you are. You, Miss Fontaine, look out of plaaace." With a raise of the dark slashes of his eyebrows, he sidestepped her.

Of all the mean-spirited, rude...*and how come he knew who she was?* Catching his arm, she was startled when her fingers connected with rock-hard muscle. He whipped around, but she held on. They faced each other again, both looking a little surprised at the electricity that crackled between them.

She caught her breath. If his arm was any indication, he certainly wasn't flabby, which meant the baggy suit wasn't covering up a weight problem. On a second glance, with some light on his face, she saw that he wasn't as old as she'd first thought, either. For a few seconds she was speechless.

"Give it up, Miss Scrooge."

"Who are you?" she asked, not letting go of him. He didn't answer, and she stared around her. Some people were looking away, trying to pretend they weren't noticing, and others were watching with great interest. Oh, darn. She'd been struggling to earn a reputation, but for good reporting, not for accosting the less fortunate than she.

"Look," she said, trying to keep her voice low and still be heard above the music and the crowd. "I was merely attempting to help out someone I thought was almost blind. I'm sorry if I offended you. But you had no right to be rude and make me the center of attention."

He snorted again and pulled back, gently forcing her to let go of him.

"You like being the center of attention, Miss Fontaine," he said. "Look at your editorial. Look at your clothes. Look at the fact that you came here at all to pick up a present. Center of attention. Yes, indeed." Clucking his tongue, he left her and walked toward the door behind the line of refreshment tables.

People tittered behind Sharon. Her jaw setting in frustration, she took a deep breath. She would not give up. This was too important to her. That man had known who she was, and Sharon had a feeling it was because he was connected to Saint Nick—if he wasn't Saint Nick himself. She had to find out, so she approached the nearest guest she saw, an elderly gentleman with a kind smile, and asked him.

"You've managed to annoy none other than Mr. Peabody," he said. "From what he's told me, he works directly for Saint Nick. The staff claims they report to him."

Which would tie in to the official statement the hotel had given her, Sharon thought. "But he's not Saint Nick?" she asked.

The man shrugged. "No one knows."

Sharon thanked him and moved on toward the door through which Mr. Peabody had disappeared. She had to find the strange man and make amends. Not that she was that worried about getting the promised present—in her heart, she knew that was too good to be true. There were no happily ever afters in life or in love. But to find Tracy Rhodes, she needed to get through to Saint Nick, and if what this man had just told her was correct, Mr. Peabody might be the only road there.

Mr. Peabody disappeared through the door leading to a long kitchen where the smell of roast beef, which had just been served, was swiftly being overpowered by the chocolate aroma of baking cakes. His mouth was set in a grim line.

That was close. He hadn't expected to run into Sharon Fontaine headlong and up-close—not quite yet, anyway. He wouldn't have guessed it was her, but the invitation she'd been holding in her hand was the color used only for the gift recipients, and he'd already met the other two.

Nick had to admit her beauty, from her high cheekbones to her rose-petal-soft lips, had also caught him off guard. When she'd stared at him, so long and hard with those sexy green eyes of hers, he'd felt some strange pull toward her. In self-defense, he'd done the only thing he could think of to push her away—acted like a jerk. He'd had to, or everything might be ruined.

Of course, Miss Fontaine had started this with her editorial, so he didn't see that he should apologize to her for anything. Imagine implying that Saint Nick had anything but the best of motives in giving away presents to people.

Well, she would learn her lesson by the end of the weekend—if she went along with what he'd proposed. Which reminded him, he'd better do a final check on the instructions for Miss Fontaine with the Reverend Dunlevy, the man who would play Santa Claus.

Snatching a Christmas cookie from a silver tray, he headed down the long aisle-like kitchen toward the far door, vowing to avoid Sharon Fontaine till she received her gift. After that, she was in for one heck of a surprise.

2

➤━◆━

Standing to the side of the crowd with a glass of wine, Sharon sighed as she watched some workers dressed like Santa's elves prepare for the second gift recipient to go on stage and sit with Santa Claus, who had arrived on schedule at nine o'clock, complete with a red suit, a full white beard and a large white sack she guessed held presents.

Her investigation wasn't going well. After almost a full hour of snooping, all she'd found out was that no one had ever met the mysterious benefactor Saint Nick. For that matter, the guests she'd spoken with claimed not to know each other, for the most part, and to be at a loss as to why they'd been invited, except that Peabody had stated that they all deserved a good time. She hadn't even found Peabody again—not that she cared to, but she needed to ask him a few questions about Saint Nick.

First, she wanted to know why the man had invited her to be a gift recipient. His motives made no sense to her at all. She had irritated him in her editorial. Why not just face her and have it out? Why give her a gift for making his life miserable? Again, the thought that Saint Nick was playing the entire town for fools grabbed hold of her and wouldn't let go.

As a drumroll sounded and Santa began to speak, Sharon finished her glass of wine, hoping it would stave off the bad attack of nerves she was getting as her time to go on stage grew closer. Despite what Mr. Peabody thought, she *didn't* like being the center of attention, and going one-on-one with Santa Claus in front of a crowd didn't thrill her, however necessary an evil it was.

Frowning, she turned her concentration to the stage. Now there was an interview she would have to do before she left tonight. Was it at all possible that the aging man dressed as Santa was Saint Nick? She supposed so, but if he denied it, how would she find out?

She listened while Santa explained to the audience that the six-year-old girl on his lap had leukemia in remission. He then bent down and asked the child what she wanted, telling her she could have anything.

"Anything?" the girl asked, fingering the lime chiffon ruffles on her dress and swinging feet donned in shiny black patent leather.

The white-bearded man nodded.

"I want flowers for my mama. My daddy can't 'ford them," the little girl said.

She had to get out of there, Sharon thought. There were too many similarities to her past here, when her mother was so sick with the cancer and they hadn't been able to afford anything, either. She preferred to keep those memories buried; she'd learned long ago she couldn't live with the pain.

Swallowing, Sharon set her empty wineglass on a sideboard and walked to the door where she'd entered. Santa was ho-ho-ho'ing again, and telling the little girl that not only would Saint Nick get her mama flowers, she would have them every day for a year, and half a year's bills paid besides, and Santa had even brought her a couple of gifts himself. The crowd clapped.

Her palms began to sweat, and she felt a sudden flush go through her as she exited the banquet hall. Her turn was next, and she felt like a sick skeptic in the middle of one of those faith healings some ministers staged on television, half praying that it was all real, but disbelieving in miracles and cynical of those swooning around her.

Suddenly weary from the onrush of emotions she'd kept buried inside for so long, Sharon leaned back against the wall in the hallway and closed her eyes. Saint Nick wasn't solving this little girl's problems. He was merely buying her a moment of happiness. That precious moment wouldn't be enough for her parents if the child's leukemia returned and killed her. They'd be left without their daughter's love, with only memories and loneliness. Sharon knew. That's all she'd been left with when her mother died. By her third foster home, she'd accepted the fact that this was the way her life was going to be, lonely and without love, and she'd quit thinking some miracle or, in this case, miracle worker, was going to come along and make her happy by rescuing her.

What made Saint Nick think he could change a damned thing about the way life was? What made him think he could be anyone's Christmas angel?

Why was Sharon Fontaine such a hard sell? Mr. Peabody, also known as Nickolaus Bonacotti, also known to only a few people as Saint Nick, stood halfway in the door, sizing up his nemesis. What he saw in front of him he really liked—dark brown hair that curved around her shoulders, green eyes that could melt steel, and a body that made him think of the words "model perfect." What he knew about her he respected—she had a brain that showed through with every article and editorial he'd read of hers—not counting the last one, of course. Normally, he might consider asking her out, but not while she was out to ruin Christmas for him by making the town think he was a fraud.

The hell of it was, he was honest-to-goodness having fun doing what he was doing, after too many years of not knowing what fun was.

Right before his father had gone off to war when Nick was ten, Vincent Bonacotti had sat Nick down and told him he'd be the man of the house until he returned. Only his dad had never come back.

For a while, Christmas had been a sad time of the year at their house. Bad enough his mom couldn't afford many presents, but worse was the fact that his sisters, too young to understand death, wished two Christmases in a row for their father to come through the door on Christmas morning. Nick had felt so powerless watching them cry on Christmas that he'd made a vow to somehow, someday, find a way to make people's Christmas wishes come true—especially the kids. He'd wanted to play Santa even then.

Anyway, he guessed he *had* pretty much become the man of the house his father had asked him to be, doing what had to be done for his mother and sisters. In return, he'd reaped the benefits, going to college and being given a lump sum from his father's life insurance that had been put into a trust fund so he could start a business. Bonacotti Industries, a toy factory, had been both a means to help support his mother and to send his sisters to school. But it had also been a natural extension of his childhood vow to play at being Santa.

When he'd decided three years ago that work wasn't enough, that he wanted to start having the fun that he'd missed as a child, it had seemed natural to play Santa to the town instead of just to his nieces and nephews.

With the help of his sister Carol, a social worker, he picked out and sent Extravaganza invitations to those people in Wheaton who went out of their way for others. Like the volunteers at the hospital, and the two women who had saved a man's life by pulling him from a burning car. People who didn't have to care, but who did anyway. To Nick, the people here tonight embodied the spirit of Christmas... with the possible exception of Sharon Fontaine.

He *was* for real, damn it. He liked making people happy, paying back some of the love he'd been given in his life. Why did Sharon Fontaine have to doubt?

She was making things very difficult. He couldn't just go up there and explain his background to her, because then she would know who he was. He might as well quit playing Saint Nick as give a reporter his true identity. People would line up in droves to get to him then, asking for favors, and he couldn't handle all the requests for help—emotionally or financially. He was already amazed that none of the gift recipients ever asked for more than he could comfortably afford. It verified his faith in people.

Yep, life had been damned good—albeit a little lonely—until Sharon Fontaine had written her editorial and started her one-woman crusade.

Inside the Extravaganza, the crowd applauded. Nick walked over to Sharon and rubbed his fingertips lightly over one of her silk-covered arms, inhaling sharply at the way touching her made him feel.

Her eyes flew open, startled, wide, *dreamy.*

"I take it back. Yes, I do," he said as Peabody. "You and that dress were made for each other."

In the light of the hallway, for a precious second or two as he stared at her with inky blue eyes, Sharon would swear Peabody could almost be good-looking and that he was flirting with her—but then he frowned, making the most awful face, and she shook her head. It had to be the wine.

"Is that an apology for your nasty remarks earlier?"

"Nope."

She pursed her lips in irritation.

"*I'm sorry* is an apology." He grinned at her. "I'm sorry."

"Was that supposed to be funny?"

"Nope. It was supposed to be an apology." His pulse pounding in his ears, Nick kept grinning at her, for some reason wanting to see her smile at him. Finally, although it seemed begrudging, somewhat more of a concession to his good nature than a smile, the edges of her lips lifted.

The child who'd gotten the gifts burst through the doorway with her parents, and Nick pointed toward the door. "Miss Fontaine. It's showtime. Yes, indeedy."

Sharon was slipping through the door as the child spotted Peabody. She half twisted to watch.

"Mr. Peabody, thank you!" the little girl said, running up and throwing her arms around him. Peabody lifted the child high and hugged her back. Then the girl's mother threw her arms around them both. "Thank Saint Nick for us, too, would you? He's been a lifesaver. We'll never forget this."

Unable to remain a minute longer, Sharon fled back to the relative darkness of the banquet hall. Santa was just leaving the stage to take a glass of water from an orange-haired elf, and a second elf was loading the girl's gifts back into Santa's huge white sack. It looked like she had a minute or so more to collect herself.

"Couldn't bear to watch them praise Saint Nick?" Mr. Peabody's nasal voice asked close to her ear. She jumped and stepped back, staring at Peabody with a lift of her eyebrow. Meeting her gaze exactly, he added, "Saint Nick gave that girl something she will always remember. Yes, he did. That family will be happier now."

"Until she dies."

"Maybe her happiness will keep her alive."

"You believe in fairy tales, Mr. Peabody. Believe me, they don't come true."

"You have a bad attitude." The smile in his magnified eyes was hypnotic, and Sharon stared at him for a long moment. There was something to this man....

The band started their third drumroll of the evening, breaking the spell.

"Ho, ho, ho! I'm looking for Sharon," Santa called from his throne in front of the band.

"Ready to feel the true spirit of Christmas, Shaaaron?" Peabody asked.

Sharon smiled smugly, whirled on one toe, and headed toward the stage.

What could possibly be behind that smile worried the hell out of Nick. Although the sexy reporter couldn't know his motivation behind inviting her here—and no matter what she might be thinking, it wasn't revenge—he was beginning to worry that, with her long stares, she was beginning to see straight through his disguise.

His thick, black glasses slipped down his nose. Seeing Sharon Fontaine's intense gaze settle upon him once more, he jerked them back up to hide his face. Not for the first time, Nick wished that there was some other way of easily disguising himself, but this was the best he could come up with. Trying to navigate with the blurred vision of the bottle bottoms was hell.

Watching the reporter now as she stood in front of Santa, her curvy body making her dress look like a white hourglass, Nick felt the same mixed wave of apprehension and attraction go through him as when she had reached out and grabbed his arm earlier. She was one attractive lady, and he liked the way she had honestly tried to help him when he'd first entered the room. She had some compassion. He could work with that.

Sharon smiled at Santa, and at the audience. Then, suddenly, she plopped down onto Santa's lap and crossed silken covered legs that didn't seem to end.

"Ho, ho, ho!" Santa said, sounding a little choked up as he raised one arm to steady her. Then he realized he was touching bare skin on her back through a cutaway section of her dress, and he yanked his hand away. "Ho, no!"

The crowd laughed, and even Nick chuckled under his breath. Sharon Fontaine was certainly full of surprises. Poor Reverend Dunlevy. Nick had promised a hefty donation to his church for his playing Santa tonight, but Sharon Fontaine had not been part of the bargain. It was a good thing Mrs. Dunlevy had stayed home.

Of its own accord, Nick's gaze flickered down to the white hose Sharon wore. He'd be dreaming about those legs tonight, he had a feeling.

"What can Saint Nick get for you, young lady?" Santa asked, his words sounding a tiny bit forced.

Sharon licked her lips. Feeling water from his slicked hair trickle down his neck, Nick shifted his weight, watching those lips, wondering what was going to come out of that rose-painted mouth. Idly, he wondered what his mother would think if he brought her home.

Now where did that thought come from? Even if he could figure out why on earth he'd want to, taking Sharon Fontaine into the Bonacotti household and maintaining his Mr. Peabody disguise would be near impossible. His mother would laugh too hard. Nah. Sharon Fontaine was a female Scrooge, and after he got her off his back, he wasn't going to have a thing to do with her. For Mr. Peabody's good.

"Well, Santa," Sharon's silky voice was saying, "you can tell Saint Nick the thing that I've been wanting most in the world..."

Nick drew his breath as her green eyes traveled over the audience and found him. She flashed him a smile, but he had no idea why. He just felt like they connected somehow, which was a mystery to him. He was dressed this way so no one would be in the least bit tempted to bother with him, and here was this female who wouldn't let go.

Maybe she was a little strange.

"Yes?" Santa—Reverend Dunlevy—prompted.

"Please tell Saint Nick," she said, loudly enough for all to hear, and in a tone that sounded strangely wistful to Nick's ears, "that I want the man of my dreams for Christmas. The love of my life. A husband."

The crowd gasped collectively, Nick the loudest of all. A human-being-type man? Now how in the hell was he supposed to come up with a husband for her? She *was* trying to ruin him. If this got out...

What the hell was he thinking, *if?* Of course it would get out, she was a reporter. If he didn't get her the man of her dreams, she would write another edi-

torial about how money couldn't buy anything
worthwhile and what a fool he was. She was going to
take all the fun out of his Christmases.

Ah, hell.

Sharon could hear the crowd's reaction and dared
another glance at Mr. Peabody to see how he'd taken
her request. Although she knew he could never grant
it for her, it had been fun to sit here like a child for a
minute or two and dream that he could. That maybe
a handsome man would now walk up on this stage and
sweep her away....

She spotted Peabody. Through his glasses, his eyes,
which had previously appeared hugely magnified, had
sharpened to two slits. Angry slits. Well, there went
that dream.... Easy come, easy go, like everything else
she'd ever held dear.

Looking at him for one long moment, he blurred
slightly, and she could almost envision him without the
glasses, the slicked hair, the ridiculous, almost clown-
ish clothes. Why did he do that to himself? The two
times she'd touched him she would have sworn he was
in shape. Fixed up, taking a little time and pride in his
looks, he might be almost passable. His nose just a
little too long, maybe, but he had a very nice
mouth...a very kissable mouth. She liked her men
with less than full lips—just like his—

"Sharon?" the gruff voice of Santa asked.

Her men? *Mr. Peabody?* Was she getting *desperate?* Good grief. And she'd smiled at him earlier! She
jerked her head around, blushing. "I'm sorry."

"Well, I was just saying that Saint Nick asked me to make a rather unusual request of you in exchange for getting your present." The microphone squealed, and he tapped it.

A catch. Certain Mr. Peabody was probably smirking, Sharon glanced back toward the spot where she'd last seen him, but he was gone, swallowed up in the crowd of red, green and gold sequins.

"Why? Have I been naughty?" she asked impishly, and was instantly sorry. That wasn't like her, either. The wine must be going to her head.

The crowd laughed at her question, and Santa waited for quiet. "Uh, hmm. Saint Nick has asked that before you get your present, you meet two of the gift recipients from last year. He will have Mr. Peabody pick you up tomorrow and escort you, and give you all the particulars. Saint Nick said to assure you this will all be to your benefit. It might even be exactly what you wanted."

Santa's bushy white eyebrows raised, as though he were asking her to be reasonable. Well, she certainly wanted to spend some time with Mr. Peabody to rack his brain about Saint Nick. "No problem, Santa."

Santa sighed audibly, and once again the crowd laughed. "Good. Assuming all goes well, you'll get your present on Christmas day."

"This we gotta see," someone said from the audience.

If the man of her dreams came to her door on Christmas, she would do a feature story, Sharon promised the crowd silently. She rose off Santa's lap. But she hoped they didn't hold their breaths. She had absolutely no faith that Saint Nick would find her a husband, but everything else was working out better than she'd hoped. She'd gotten a free ticket to see Mr. Peabody again, and that was half her battle. Leaning down, she planted a quick kiss on Santa's cheek. "Can I talk to you when you're free?"

"Ho, ho, ho!" Santa said. "No!"

That's what he thought. Stepping off the stage, Sharon was surprised when no one approached her. But what had she expected? There were no reporters here, except for her. Actually, it was all a bit of a relief not to have to answer anyone's questions. One more interview, and she was free to go home and write down and review all she'd learned tonight, so she would be prepared for her editor's cross-examination on Monday.

The band filtered back on stage and struck up something from the top ten. So, Mr. Peabody had some up-to-date tastes after all. Amazing. Sharon watched as Santa called Merry Christmas to everyone and left through a side door. Waiting a minute so she didn't appear too conspicuous, she hurried out the same door and glanced up a long hall.

Apparently, Santa wasn't going to change into street clothes. Still in his suit, he'd already reached the exit and was starting to push through the glass door that led to the parking lot. She was too near the party to yell—she would call attention to herself, and that was the last thing she wanted to do. Mr. Peabody might have her thrown out.

By the time she had run a few feet, Santa was already outside, and in the few seconds it took her to reach the door and swing it open to a blast of cold air, he was unlocking an early model van. Some sleigh, she thought, noting the sunshine yellow flowers painted on the side.

"Santa, wait a minute!"

"Sorry, I'm married!" The grizzled, white-haired man waved and climbed into the driver's seat.

"Ho, ho, ho," she said under her breath. Running toward his vehicle, she shivered in her thin dress. If he were Saint Nick, she couldn't let him get away.

Too late by seconds, she did manage to jot down his license number on the small pad of paper she kept in her purse. She had a memory like a sieve, especially when it came to numbers, so she had to write down everything. But with the license number, she'd have an address by Monday afternoon, so she had a backup plan starting to gel, just in case Mr. Peabody didn't come through with Saint Nick.

She ripped off the piece of paper and waved it once triumphantly in the air, only to have it snatched from her fingers.

"Hey!" she said, spinning around. Mr. Peabody, all six feet or so of him, stood behind her. His hand was just coming out of the pocket of his cavernous pants, his fingers empty.

"I want that back!" With a giddy sense of desperation, she lunged for his pants' pocket, but he easily pulled her wrist up and away from him. She pushed down, trying again to get to his pocket for that number.

"I wouldn't go hunting in there, Ms. Fontaine," he said, his voice whiskey-smooth.

"Afraid I wouldn't find anything of value?" she asked just as smoothly. "Apart from my note, that is?"

They stared at each other for a few seconds, well illuminated under a parking lot light. A droplet of water rolled down his forehead as she watched him, trying to think of what was suddenly different about him since the last time they'd come face-to-face.

Then she had it—his voice. Gone was the nasalness. In its place had been a mellow, rich timbre—or had she just imagined that? Once again, the scent of that same sexy men's cologne she'd detected earlier wafted toward her, throwing her concentration. It was not the type of cologne a man like Peabody would put on. Expensive, sensual. No, it just wasn't for real. It had to be the wine—the first she'd had since college—making her imagine all this.

Then she recalled what she had just said to him. Good Lord, what was wrong with her? That was it, she vowed, she was never drinking again. Now she was hearing and smelling and *saying* things. Next thing she knew, she would start thinking *Mr. Peabody* was the man of her dreams.

Giving up on her paper—God only knew how deep those oversize pockets were, and she *was not* about to grope him—she started back toward the hotel, planning to get her coat and go. She'd never been one for parties.

"Shaaaron," Mr. Peabody called, the nasality back. Scowling slightly, she turned to see what he wanted.

"I'll pick you up at the newspaper at ten tomorrow. To fulfill the terms of Saint Nick's agreement. Must do."

"You sure I'll be safe with you?"

"I was asking myself the same thing about you. Yes, I was."

"I'm sure you were," Sharon said easily. The nasality and his peculiar speech patterns were back. Mr. Peabody was hiding something, she thought. But what? An education? A criminal background?

No, she was just imagining things. She shook her head. What a night. It was a good thing she didn't have to explain this to anyone. No one would believe it. A man who was something out of a "disaster date" game had latched himself on to her for probably most of tomorrow, depending on how long it took to visit last year's two recipients and how long it took for her to milk all the information about Saint Nick she could out of him.

Freezing, she rubbed her arms and concentrated on getting warm. She was halfway down the hall heading toward the cloakroom next to the Extravaganza before she realized the significance of what she had just agreed to. Mr. Peabody was going to pick her up *at the Tribune.*

Bolting back the way she'd come in, she shoved open the glass door and surveyed the parking lot. Peabody should have followed her inside, but he hadn't. She hurried back to the party, but he wasn't there, either.

She stood next to the door, her jaw set. During *the season,* they worked at almost full staff on Saturdays. All her co-workers were going to see him. She *could* explain till she ran out of words that he was a source for a story, but that wouldn't stop the other reporters from making her life miserable. Once Mr. Peabody showed up and asked for her, the teasing would never stop. Why did everything have to be such a battle?

For the first time she wondered if she had done the right thing wishing for the man of her dreams. It would be nice to get her wish, but she doubted such a man existed. She had too many stipulations.

For one, he'd have to be someone who respected her needs and who wanted her to be happy—even when it wasn't quite convenient for him. She'd lived too long subject to other people's convenience. Secondly, he would not dream of running off when faced with responsibility—like her father had. And most of all, the man of her dreams would be someone who loved her not for who she was, but *despite* who she was, so the love would last. God but she didn't want to live without love in her life forever.

Shivering, blinking back the heavy feeling of tears in her eyes, Sharon shook her head. Having the man of her dreams was too much to expect out of life. Just like wishing for her mother to live had been. What she should have asked for tonight was to meet Saint Nick. Now that would have saved her a lot of time and energy.

But she'd missed her chance, she thought, wiping her eyes with the palm of her hand, and now she would just have to find him the hard way.

3

---→←---

The next morning Sharon paced the front lobby of the *Tribune* with her arms across her chest, as though body language alone could ward off who she knew was coming. Even so, when Mr. Peabody's nasal tones rang across the room, calling her name, she cringed. A quick glance told her the coast was clear of her co-workers. Only the receptionist noticed him, and gawking though she was, she would keep quiet, thanks to the ten dollars Sharon had slipped her. She'd better.

"He's only a source," she reminded herself. Rushing forward, she grabbed Mr. Peabody's arm and pulled him behind her, shoving open the door and practically yanking on him to make him move more quickly. "Where's your car?"

"I'm hurt. Yes, I am," he whined. "I thought I would meet your friennnds."

Sharon grimaced. He had pulled the last word out so long she'd considered offering to pay for speech lessons. "Mr. Peabody, where is your car?"

"Have to explain. Got a small problem. This is—"

"Mr. Peabody!" she said from between clenched teeth. "Just show me a car!" *Before somebody comes and you ruin my life.*

He pointed to a Volkswagen Bug parked a few cars down that had to be thirty years old—and looked every minute of it.

"Does it run?" she asked, unable to contain the long sigh that followed her words.

He opened his mouth.

"Never mind. Of course it runs, or you wouldn't have gotten over here." Taking his arm again, she hurried him toward the car. If anyone saw her . . .

"What's your hurry?" he asked, stopping by the passenger side right next to her. "Worried somebody might see you with me? I know I'm strange-looking. Bothers some people. Yes, it does." He sounded apologetic.

Sharon stared up at him. Instantly she felt ashamed of herself. He was a human being, after all. He couldn't help being odd. Or having a poor speaking voice.

"You aren't that bad-looking. You have great possibilities." Reaching up, she brushed away two droplets of water hanging right above his thick, dark brown eyebrows. He pulled back at her touch and, at the same time, stunned, she almost yanked her hand back. She didn't know what she had been expecting, but it wasn't the almost comforting feeling of warmth that had radiated down her fingers into her heart. . . . She stared up at Mr. Peabody, wondering how he could be so abnormal, yet affect her so strangely.

She would have to think about that later. Right now, she had to get him out of sight. "The keys, Mr. Peabody?" she said to nudge him into action.

He dipped his hands into his pockets, and then into his jacket. "Oh, boy. Oh, boy. My keys. I think I lost them. Can we take your car?"

"Thank you, Lord," she muttered, her voice filled with relief.

"What?"

"Certainly, we can. Come this way." She turned and headed toward the corner and around, not watching to see if he followed. He would.

Sensing him steps behind her, she hurried her pace. Once they were in her car, she could start interviewing him. Already, on the street, they were attracting any number of stares, and her cheeks flushed hotly. Dipping her fingers into her pocket, she fished out her keys and had them ready to unlock the passenger door for him. "I have to let it warm up a few minutes."

"No prob-lem," he said, his voice ringing out. A couple of kids passing by snickered and pointed, and she practically dove into the driver's side. Sharon made a mental note to write her friend Catherine and ask if she'd ever suffered through anything like this as a reporter.

They sat in silence for a few minutes, broken only when she saw that his knees were stuck up against the dash. She told him how to push the seat back so he'd be more comfortable. When he gave her directions to the first place, what he claimed was a home in the still respectable, lower income section of town, she pulled out into traffic. The one-way streets downtown were a pain. She'd have to go down one street, cut over two because of construction, and head back toward the *Tribune* building.

She remained quiet another few minutes as she waited at two separate lights, trying to think of the best questions to ask him. It seemed kind of blunt to just blurt out, "Who is Saint Nick?" Besides, she didn't think he'd tell her.

"Are you ashamed?" he asked quietly, breaking into her thoughts. "To be seen with me?"

"Of course not!" she said. She wasn't lying, exactly. Ashamed wasn't the word. More like *mortified*.

"I have great possibilities, you said. In the looks department?"

Resting her hands on the steering wheel as she waited for the traffic to clear so she could make a right turn, she glanced over at him. The poor man had literally no self-esteem. He looked like an oversize schoolboy with his brown socks showing below his too-short pants, and his wrists exposed by his too-short jacket sleeves. But his dark brown hair was thick and shiny now that the heater had dried it out some. His glasses had slid down just a bit on his nose, and she could see black eyelashes, which shaded what looked like a promise of gorgeous eyes a tad lighter than inky blue. She leaned sideways a bit for a closer view.

He pushed his glasses up high on his nose with a jerk. Embarrassed, she pretended she had been reaching for the radio.

"Well, your hair is perfect without all that water you spritz on it," she said. That was the truth. It was all feathered at the sides, and seemed to whisper an invitation to run her fingers through it that very minute.

What was she thinking?

"Hair's too thick," he said. "Water keeps it flat. Otherwise I look like a girl."

She shook her head. Under no circumstances would anyone mistake Mr. Peabody for a girl. Never.

Making the right-hand turn, she drove past the newspaper building, glancing at it to see if she knew anyone coming out who might spot her with Mr. Peabody. Then she noticed something wrong. Her mouth flying open, she jerked the wheel to the right and squealed into a parking space.

"What?" Mr. Peabody yelled, still holding on to the dashboard as she reached for the button that would unlock their doors.

"Your car's been stolen," she said. She couldn't believe this. Not more than ten minutes ago it had been parked in the open space four cars behind them.

"Stolen?" He sounded confused.

"Somebody must have seen you lose your keys," she suggested. She was about to add "or hotwired your car," but before she could, Mr. Peabody patted his pocket with a confused look on his face. He didn't say anything, but she heard the unmistakable clink of keys. She eyed him steadily, and he suddenly looked flustered.

"If you had the keys," Sharon asked, "then why didn't you drive us in your car?"

"No driver's license. Eyesight too bad."

"If you can't see, how did you drive the Bug here?"

"Carefully."

She groaned. He was covering up something, and he had her so bewildered, she wasn't even sure what.

He threw up his hands. "Ah, you caught me in a lie. Bug wasn't my car. Came in taxi."

She took a deep breath. "Why didn't you tell me that to begin with?"

He grinned. "You said 'show me a car.' I showed you. Good one, huh? Classic. Like my suit."

Sharon leaned her head against the steering wheel and closed her eyes.

"Sharon? Are you all right?"

His voice suddenly had a different sound to it, velvet and smooth again, like she'd thought she'd heard last night. He sounded different from the cut-and-dried Mr. Peabody, more like a man, like he was really concerned about her instead of just doing his job. Maybe, she thought, her eyes still closed, just maybe when she raised her head up and looked at him, Mr. Peabody would suddenly be a gorgeous hunk, and the sound of caring in his voice would be real, and she wouldn't have to wind up like her mom, alone, with none of her wishes answered.

"Sharon?" The same velvet-hot voice, like a slow sip of the finest whiskey, called her name again.

She jerked her head up and looked at him. She was still in her nightmare. Mr. Peabody himself sat next to her, in the same suit, with the same glasses that he'd been wearing last night. The green-and-red striped tie was gone, though. The one he wore now was actually a dark brown that matched the long brown pinstripes in the plaid.

"Nice tie," she said softly.

"I dressed up for you," he said, and snorted right before laughing, as though it were funny. "Drive on, Rudolph," he added, as though talking to a chauffeur—or Santa's head reindeer.

Putting the car in gear, Sharon wondered how to explain to Harley that with this assignment, she felt like she was in some sort of flaky war of the minds with this man, and she very definitely deserved hazard pay.

Mr. Peabody gave her the same answers to her gentle probing that she'd learned he'd given everyone at the Extravaganza. What questions he didn't answer, he neatly evaded. Fifteen unproductive minutes later Sharon was being given a tour of a neat, white, frame house in a working-class neighborhood, the place given to Donnya Farmer by Saint Nick last year. The scent of candy apples greeted Sharon in the kitchen, and from somewhere in the back of the house echoed children's laughter. It was a happy, though modest, home.

"I just asked Santa for a house for me and my three kids, and Saint Nick, through Mr. Peabody—" she stopped speaking and grinned at Peabody, who returned a bashful smile "—arranged for this one." Donnya, an attractive African American woman somewhere in her early twenties, spread her arms wide. "I live here rent free, just pay the property taxes and the utilities, and I save my money. My kids are gonna go to college.''

''Wonderful.'' How interesting, Sharon thought, that Saint Nick had set the woman in a working-class neighborhood. ''Were you disappointed at all that the house wasn't larger or fancier?''

Mr. Peabody snorted, and Donnya leveled her with a look. ''Why would I want to be movin' up into a different neighborhood where nobody knows me and I don't have any friends? Here, I was able to open a business.''

''A business?''

Donnya nodded proudly and gestured for Sharon to follow her down a hall to a back room. As they approached, Sharon could hear the children more clearly as they giggled. Then a tinkling piano and a lovely, if shaky, soprano struck up a rousing ''Rudolph the Red-Nosed Reindeer,'' and a chorus of small voices, full of joy, joined in. Sharon winced.

''Welcome to Donnya's Day Haven.'' Donnya pushed the slightly ajar door open wider, and Sharon peeked into the room. On the thick carpeting sat five preschoolers, grinning and singing their hearts out. On a nearby table, gaily decorated with a small Christmas tree and twinkling lights, were the candy apples she'd smelled in the kitchen. Stuffed animals sat in every corner, and all over the walls were huge, hand-made cloth letters in shades of calico.

''Looks more like a Donnya's Day *Heaven* to me,'' Sharon complimented. If she won Donnya's confidence, she might be able to get more information out of her.

"Thank you. I think the children agree with you." Donnya waved at the woman at the piano and shut the door. "The day care's for low-income families, so the mothers can work. Usually I'm in there, but my mama volunteered to watch the kids while I talked to you," she said.

"Did Saint Nick ask you to open up the day care?" Sharon asked.

"Heavens, no! When he gave me this house, I wanted to put something back into the community. I can't explain it. It was something I had to do—help others like Saint Nick helped me."

"Have you ever met the man?"

Donnya shook her head.

Sharon glanced at Mr. Peabody, knowing he wasn't going to like her next question, but needing to ask, anyway. "Saint Nick doesn't get a cut of the business, does he?"

Donnya looked shocked, and her coffee brown eyes, which had been so calm during the whole time she'd been talking to Sharon, suddenly flashed steamy brown. "How could you say such a thing? Saint Nick has to be the most caring individual in this whole city."

"Yes, he is," Mr. Peabody piped in.

Sharon scowled at him. "I didn't mean anything bad by the question. It's just that I find it hard to believe anyone is so generous in this day and age. To give like he does and expect nothing in return."

"Where've you been, Miss Fontaine?" Donnya asked. "There's good people out there, all over, just like there's bad. The difference is, the bad want to get noticed, and being bad's the only way they know how. The good don't. They just want to see others happy.''

Her homespun observation made sense, but Sharon didn't think it was that simple. "What about you, Ms. Farmer? Wouldn't the money for the house have been better spent getting you a college education so you could get a better paying job?"

Donnya threw up her hands in total disgust. "I love what I do. I'm making money at it. It ain't a lot, but I'm real happy, right here. So what's wrong with being happy, Miss Fontaine?"

"Sharon doesn't know how," Mr. Peabody said. "No, she doesn't."

This was all too much. Her jaw set stiffly, Sharon thanked the woman and left the house, not caring if Mr. Peabody followed her or not. But of course, he did.

"Nice lady, huh?" Mr. Peabody said, getting in the passenger's side.

"Very," Sharon said. She buckled her seat belt and waited for him to put his on. "Why did Saint Nick want me to meet her?" Her words were clipped, but maybe her tone would anger Mr. Peabody into revealing something. She had to get some kind of story out of this, and it was getting harder and harder when all she wanted to do was ditch Mr. Peabody—permanently.

"You weren't very nice to Saint Nick, in your article," Mr. Peabody said. "No, you weren't. He is sincere. He wants to help people. Didn't Donnya prove that?"

She wasn't admitting to anything until she got the whole story behind Saint Nick. Putting the key in the ignition, she said, "Donnya was a very nice, hard-working young woman, who is going to be in that house till she dies, and probably have her kids be in that house with their kids. She can't put them through college on a baby-sitter's wage. Saint Nick has changed nothing in her life. She would've been better off if she'd stayed in her apartment and used the money to put herself through school. She seemed smart enough."

Mr. Peabody let out a long whistle. "Somebody is cynical. Yes, indeedy. Don't you believe in hopes and dreams?"

"I believe in hard work and definitive, reachable goals."

"Then what about the man of your dreams you asked Saint Nick for?"

"A slip of sanity," she said. Which was exactly what her request had been. No one was going to hand her anything in life, least of all love. She was a fool to wish otherwise.

"Nooo, Sharon," Mr. Peabody said, shaking his head. "Not a slip of sanity. More like a slip of the heart."

Sharon wished she could scream. Suddenly, she re-alized why none of the guests at the Extravaganza could get anything out of Mr. Peabody. He didn't talk to you; he talked *around* you. She had to get a grip on this situation fast.

She whipped her head around. "What about Tracy Rhodes?"

"What about her?" Mr. Peabody asked evenly, his smile never leaving his face.

"Where is she?"

"Somewhere between content and happy, I think."

He was the most exasperating man! "Are you going to answer any of my questions, Mr. Peabody?"

"When you ask a happy one. Told you last night—you need a positive attitude, Miss Fontaine. Get a positive attitude, and the answers you want will come. Guarantee it."

"Oh, you do, do you?" Sharon stopped at a light and raised her eyebrow. "You didn't say. Where to next?"

"Wheaton's Community Service Center. It's almost eleven-thirty. Quite time for us to be there."

She made a right at the next corner. A beeper went off, shrill in the otherwise quiet car. Mr. Peabody pulled it out of his pocket and nodded. "Yes, it's mine. Sorry. Have to go. Important lunch engagement arranged after all."

"Where can I drop you?" Sharon asked, watching him out of the corner of her eye.

Did he look alarmed at her question, or was it her imagination?

"In front of the *Tribune*. I'll get a cab."

"I'll be happy to take you wherever you need to go—"

He grinned. "Happy, happy. See, Miss Fontaine? I'm getting through to you. I'll make a Christmas believer out of you yet."

"Bah, hum—" She stopped herself and glanced at Mr. Peabody. He was grinning.

He was without a doubt the most frustrating individual she had ever run across. She had handled high-pressure interviews with the crusty mayor with ease, but there was something about this cloddish man that kept her constantly flustered.

Leaning forward, Mr. Peabody turned on the radio and switched stations until he found "Santa Claus is Coming to Town," and began to sing along in his nasal, off-key voice with great exuberance and a look of childlike joy on his face. She glanced at him twice while she was driving, and the look never left him. Not wanting to change his mood, she didn't bother to say anything about his singing until she pulled up in front of the *Tribune* building. To her amazement, she found herself smiling at him. Cordially.

"You really do like Christmas, don't you, Mr. Peabody?"

He winked at her, then grinned, showing his perfect teeth. Then, without an iota of warning, he swooped down and planted a kiss on her lips. Shocked, she let his lips linger against hers for what only was seconds, she was sure, but felt like an eternity.

A pleasant, wonderful eternity.

He jerked back and slid out of the car with the sure, easy movements of a born athlete. "I'll call you, Shaaaron," he promised, chuckling.

Her heart thumping madly with shock, Sharon watched him as he walked down the street, attracting stares and surprised looks from the strollers and the passersby. She'd let Mr. Peabody kiss her!

She started giggling, and for the life of her, she didn't know why. She was suddenly very happy, but she had no reason to be. She hadn't gotten any kind of story out of this. Mr. Peabody had kissed her, and she had enjoyed it.

It could have been worse, she thought. At least he hadn't snorted after the kiss.

Maybe she wasn't getting out enough. Wait till she called Catherine and told her about this interview!

Her eyes opened wide. What on earth was she doing just sitting there? Mr. Peabody had stunned her so badly she wasn't thinking. He was on foot; she could easily catch up in her car to the point where she found him, and then hang back until someone picked him up or until he got to his destination. Either way, she was sure to learn something about him. Maybe he would even take her right to Saint Nick.

When he was far enough away, Nick ducked between the steel noise barriers around the first pay phone he could find and called his office. He hadn't lied to Sharon. He did have a business lunch that had depended on whether or not the possible buyer could make it, and he'd told his secretary to beep him. But he'd hated having to leave Sharon.

After hearing her request for the man of her dreams last night, he'd kicked a wall or two in private, and then decided the only way he could grant her wish was to attach himself to her until he figured out what kind of man she needed. Then he could try to match her up with one of his employees. His solution was feeble, but it was the only one he could come up with.

Upon spending some time with her, he'd figured out that Sharon Fontaine was hurting, deep inside. The way she was now...well, suffice it to say he didn't know any saints to match her up with, and he figured that was the only type of man who would put up with her. He had decided that finding her a willing man would be easier if he could remind her how to be happy, so he'd kissed her.

He'd befuddled the reporter when he'd done that, he knew. But he'd also been surprised at how good it had felt when their lips had touched and she'd kissed back a little. Underneath her cold, calculating exterior crackled fire. There was a warmth to Sharon that was buried under a rock of cynicism. He wondered if he could unearth enough of her heart to make her believe he was for real. He wondered if anyone could.

At least now that he knew Ms. Fontaine had coldly set out to get Saint Nick's attention through her editorial so that she could try to find the missing Tracy Rhodes, he had an idea of what he was up against.

The last thing he wanted was for a reporter to get her hands on Tracy. As Mr. Peabody, he'd promised the young woman her wish would be kept secret, and he'd stick by it. No matter how fond he was becoming of Sharon Fontaine, he'd have to find a way of stopping her before she got her story.

4

The way Mr. Peabody was dressed, Sharon thought, he was like a lighthouse beacon in a foggy night. Spotting him immediately, she pulled into a parking place on the street, watching as he left a phone booth about a hundred feet away and bent his tall frame into the back seat of a cab. She bit back a smile at what the driver must be thinking of his new fare. Cabdrivers dealt with all kinds of people, she knew, but Mr. Peabody was one in a million.

She followed the yellow cab three blocks over and one block down to the town's Industrial Drive. They passed the glassworks and a plastics manufacturer before the cab turned into the parking lot of Bonacotti Industries, a toy factory if she remembered correctly. Not immense, the parking lot was at least big enough so that she couldn't be seen from the cab when she slid her car into a parking place to the front left. Grabbing her purse, she headed toward where the cab had dropped off Peabody, directly next to the double-story rear of the factory.

Peabody disappeared through a side entrance. Thankful she chose to work primarily in comfortable knit pants and sensible flats, Sharon ran so she wouldn't lose him, entering a stairwell foyer of sorts. The sound of feet shuffling above her head directed her up the steps to a heavy fire door that opened into a long hall. Through the thick glass, she saw Mr. Peabody enter a nearby doorway.

After a minute, she took a chance that Peabody wouldn't rush right out again and slipped into the hallway herself to check where he'd disappeared to. It was the men's room. Deciding to wait, she hurried back to relative obscurity behind the glass fire door.

Minutes ticked by, and she wondered exactly what she was going to do when Peabody came out. If she followed him, she ran the risk of someone confronting her and throwing her out. On the other hand, he might go directly to his boss's office.

Excitement coursed through her. She could actually be minutes away from meeting the real Saint Nick and getting her break-out story. The adrenaline rush was terrific, just like Catherine had told her it would be.

Someone exited the men's room, and Sharon sucked in her breath. Shaking her head in confusion, she stared, her view slightly blurred by the glass. Physically, the man could be Peabody; the hair and the height were the same. But the glasses were gone, and he was wearing pleated pants and a jewel blue, polo-type shirt that stretched over his upper body like a knit glove. He ambled down the hall with an easy, relaxed swing to his movements, where Peabody walked swiftly. A few feet before the end of the hall, he reached another door and turned left, disappearing once more from view.

Could something have happened to Peabody? He *had* gone in and never come out. It was Saturday, and if these were offices, the place was probably deserted. There were high-class burglars and murderers, and it was a nutty world and anything was possible... and...

All right, she admitted, she *was* worried about him. He was so innocent, so unaware of the bad things that could happen to him.

Pulling open the door, she slipped through and ran toward the men's room. Once more she hesitated, but then she yanked open the door and peeked around the front barrier to see if Peabody was lying mugged on the floor.

Nobody was in front of the row of urinals, thank goodness. Bending, she glanced under the stalls, and then checked inside each open door, just to make sure. Empty. Frowning, she glanced at the sinks, and to the left of them, at a huge supply cabinet. When she saw that, she suddenly knew what had happened to Peabody.

Sure enough, on one side of the cabinet floor there were two paper sacks, containing a plaid suit, glasses, brown tie—everything except a set of underwear and Peabody himself. Either Peabody had become invisible, or the hunk she'd seen coming out of here minutes before had seen fit to disguise himself as Saint Nick's representative. What better reason than because he was Saint Nick?

She half smiled at the thought of the mystery man of Wheaton fooling everybody that way. Then she realized that the hunk she'd seen had been the same man who'd kissed her and sent her senses reeling, and suddenly she wasn't so amused any longer. The man—Saint Nick—knew she was a reporter, and he'd been playing her for a fool.

But what to do about it? She still didn't have a name, or a real identity, just the memory of a slightly blurred face, and the clothes he was wearing at the moment. She had to learn his identity before he changed back into Peabody.

Pulling open the men's room door, she almost crashed into a sandy-haired deliveryman. He raised his eyebrow toward the word Men on the door and then glared at her as if he were a guardian of a sacred fort.

She couldn't resist. "Yes, I read it right. Be careful. I was a man when I went in there."

"Huh?"

Waiting till she slipped past him to grin widely, she walked authoritatively down the hall until she reached the solid door she believed Saint Nick had gone through.

Aha!

The words Nickolaus Bonacotti, President, were in neat gold letters. Pausing only for a second, she opened the door and entered. Inside was a typical front office, with a secretary at a catercornered desk, and a short hallway leading to three other doors, all of which were closed.

The fortyish secretary looked up from her computer terminal and smiled. "Yes? May I help you?"

"I'd like to see Mr. Bonacotti, please." She needed to confront him. Once she saw his face close up, she was sure he would have to admit to being Peabody.

But then again, he didn't have to admit to being Saint Nick.

"I'm sorry, he's on the telephone," the secretary said pleasantly, indicating a lit button on her desk phone with a red-painted nail. "When he gets off, he's going to have a meeting with a client that might last quite a while. Would you like an appointment?"

"How soon?"

The woman leafed through her calendar. "Wednesday afternoon, two o'clock is the earliest he has open. He's always really busy around Christmastime."

"I'll just bet," she muttered. She would be seeing Peabody before Wednesday, she knew.

"No, thank you," she added, turning to leave.

"Can I tell him who inquired?" the secretary asked.

Sharon shook her head and strolled out as though she hadn't a care in the world. She was halfway to her car when it occurred to her that perhaps she'd been lucky not getting to see Saint Nick right away. Maybe a confrontation *wouldn't* be best. Nick Bonacotti could simply deny knowing what she was talking about. If she could get into his office somehow, she could nose around the files to see if she could come up with some definitive proof of Saint Nick's being Nick Bonacotti, and the whereabouts of Tracy Rhodes. Then he'd be trapped, and he'd have to give her a story.

By the time she was in her car, she thought she just might know the way to pull off her escapade. The thing she had to decide was when. She still had one more gift recipient to see with Peabody, and she wanted to have some fun with him. He deserved it for pulling off this scam.

But try as she might, she couldn't rid her mind of the image of the man Mr. Peabody was underneath his disguise. She kept imagining him as Nick Bonacotti, sitting next to her earlier and leaning over to kiss her. He hadn't had to do that to win her over to Saint Nick's point of view. After all, he'd been posing as Mr. Peabody, who supposedly was only an employee and therefore would be unaffected by any exposé. There was no reason for him to kiss her that she could figure, except one—he'd wanted to. The thought made her almost breathless with anticipation.

Anticipation, yes—but a little bit of fear, too. What if she found she actually liked Saint Nick? What if she let herself *want* one more time, and it didn't work out? She didn't know if she could stand any more disappointment in her life where men were concerned. How much easier it was to just not care.

Sharon stared blindly into the vehicle-filled parking lot. Where Nick Bonacotti was concerned, for the first time in a long time she had no clear picture in her mind of exactly what was going to dictate her next move—her brain or her timid, life-scarred heart.

On Monday, Sharon gave her editor a quick run-down on the party. When she told him she'd asked Saint Nick for a man, Harley turned purple—strange, she thought, with his red hair. Sheer, utter waste, Harley called it. But he quickly recovered when she told him she had gotten some information on one of the prior year's recipients and would be meeting the other soon, so she was making progress toward a story. She didn't bother to tell him she'd trailed Mr. Peabody to a business and was going to follow it up. He would want to know all about that, and Sharon wasn't certain she was ready to tell.

That afternoon with the sole intent of getting information, she went down to Bonacotti Industries and filled out an application to work on the cleaning staff, using a false name and background. By the time she finished talking to the sweet personnel receptionist, she knew all the details of the job, including the fact that because of the Christmas season and overtime they were all working later than usual. After doing the offices, the staff all went to the cafeteria downstairs for a break, usually around nine.

Armed with that knowledge, Sharon thought on her way back to the office, all she had to do was bide her time and wait for Saint Nick to make the next move. When the time was right to go after verifiable proof at Bonacotti Industries, she'd know it.

This was not what he'd expected. Nick, dressed as Mr. Peabody, paced in the hallway in front of Sharon Fontaine's apartment, waiting for her to answer his second knock. He had called her this morning, inviting her to go see the other gift recipient, the first free moment he'd had since Saturday. When he'd offered to meet her at the *Tribune* again, she'd insisted he come to her place. He had to wonder if she was up to something.

On his third stride up the hall, she finally answered his knock. "Hi, stranger."

He whipped around. She was dressed in a bottle green satiny shirt that intensified the green of her eyes and outlined every sweet curve of her upper body. She *was* up to something. Suddenly Nick found he was intrigued. He wondered what was driving her so hard that she would resort to—dare he voice it— *seduction?*

"Miss Fontaine—" His voice broke.

"Shaaaron," she reminded him, drawing out her name the same way he had. "Won't you come in? I'm almost ready."

Her hips were clad in faded blue jeans that were molded to her, and he couldn't take his eyes off them as she walked inside, straight through a small living room into an even tinier kitchen. Sticking his hands into the pockets of Peabody's yellow plaid suit, he stopped at the doorway, already feeling too boxed in with her in that outfit. The place was tiny, and she wasn't helping.

"I was just going to have some coffee before we leave." Sharon grabbed a mug off the sideboard and smiled at him. "Join me, Peabody? It'll heat you up."

She was doing that all by herself. "That would be nice," he said, remembering to talk in a singsong fashion in the nick of time. He'd already slipped up once too often in front of her. He couldn't have her suspecting him.

She turned to him and raised her eyes. "Sugar?" she asked, running the tip of her tongue over her lips.

Oh, God. It took him a few seconds to realize she meant *in his coffee.*

"Black," he croaked.

"Sure." She smiled and put down the empty tea-spoon she was holding. It clinked against the steel of the sink. Walking over to a two-seater kitchen table at the other end of the kitchen, she set down the mug.

"Have a seat," she invited.

He did, watching as she poured herself a cup. He wasn't really ready to go back outside quite yet; an icy wind had settled over Wheaton, and his wet hair felt frozen in parts.

She remained standing by the counter and took a sip from her cup, her pink lips curving around the rim. Was it chance that her other arm draped just under her breasts, flattening the material to show every con-tour?

Or was she flirting with him?

In the plain light of day, on her own turf, Sharon's sexual magnetism seemed intense. Or were all those day and night dreams he'd been having about her throwing her every movement way out of propor-tion?

He shook his head, shivering, unsure whether it was because of his hair or her. Gulping down a scalding mouthful of coffee, he sighed with contentment at the extra warmth flowing through him, but in a few sec-onds he shivered again.

"I think I have the cure for what ails you, Pea-body," she said softly, disappearing around the cor-ner. He heard the squeak of a door being opened, and then she returned, holding a blow-dryer.

"Oh, no," he squeaked, sensing trouble and trying to lurch up out of his seat. He didn't make it. She blocked him. If he pushed against her, his head would go right into her breasts. Even now, he could feel their softness brushing against the back of his head as she plugged the dryer into the wall socket.

"Now just sit back and relax."

"Impossible!"

"Sure it is, Peabody. You just need to change your attitude." She smiled down at him. She was still blocking his way to freedom, and the last thing he wanted to do was touch her to push her out of the way. He was too afraid it would mean the end of his resolve.

Four of her fingers pressed against the nape of his neck—he could feel every single one. A low hum began as she clicked on the dryer, and a hot stream of air started melting the ice cube his head had become.

"Why must you touch me?" he asked, referring to her fingers on his neck. Those damnably soft fingers that moved ever so slightly when he voiced the question. He remembered once more just in time he wasn't Nick now and added, Peabody-like, "Yes, why must you?"

"The heat might burn your skin. I wouldn't want to have you *unprotected.*"

He heard an implication to her words he was positive she didn't mean. But then those gentle fingers moved up and drifted through his hair.

"Close your eyes, Peabody. Enjoy." Her voice was a caress of air close to his ear.

His nerves crackled, and he leapt out of his skin when her fingers drifted down over his ears. *What* was she doing? Not for one minute did he believe this was all to protect his *tender* skin.

"Uh, Miss Fontaine—"

"Sharon."

"Please don't do this," he begged. "We have to go. Yes, we do."

Nick started to pull away, but her fingers went through his hair like a comb and tugged his head backward until he was looking up at the undercurve of her breast. The dryer landed up on the table, and before he quite knew what was happening, her free hand reached down to unbutton the top button of his white shirt. She slipped it free and twirled the hair on his chest with her fingertips.

"What are you doing?" he yelped, sucking in a breath and yanking free so hard this time she was forced to let him go. Once on his feet, he stared at her in disbelief. All this because of one little kiss? The woman was desperate, Nick thought. He'd made a big mistake. Some people you had to leave alone. Like in that movie with Michael Douglas where that woman pursued him—

"It took me a while, but I finally understand," she said softly. Framed by thick, dark lashes, her green eyes held an invitation that he almost couldn't resist. "Saint Nick means for *you* to be the man of my dreams."

"Oh, no, he doesn't!" He backed up.

She ran her finger under the edge of her neckline, exposing an expanse of soft white skin above her collarbone. Nick wanted, badly, to put his lips right there—

She had him crazy! Sharon Fontaine wasn't the right woman for him. She was a one-way ticket to catastrophe.

"How do you know he doesn't intend for me to have you?" she asked. "Because you're Saint Nick?"

"I most certainly am not!" What was she basing that on? He backed up again, his eyes narrowing suspiciously.

Her eyes were half shut as she regarded him with amusement. "I'm harmless, Peabody."

"As an alleycat. Yes. A female alleycat."

"Are you afraid of me, or of being found out?"

"Nothing to find out." Everything to be afraid of. She was confusing the hell out of him, and he wanted to escape to figure out what he was going to do. He still had to throw her off Tracy Rhodes's trail, so he couldn't just change back to Nick Bonacotti and disappear. He sure wasn't about to drop his Christmas celebrations unless it was absolutely necessary, which meant he had to find some way around Sharon Fontaine. He turned toward her front door.

"If you aren't the man of my dreams, then why did you kiss me the other day?"

"I take the Fifth. Yes, I do." Was that what this was all about? A simple kiss? No way. Sharon was too smart for that. She was fishing, hoping to get him sidetracked so he would slip up somehow. She suspected he was Saint Nick, which meant the end to face-to-face confrontations.

He jerked open her door, but stopped when he felt her hand on his arm.

"What about our visit to the last gift recipient?"

"I'll call you. I promise. Tomorrow." By then, he would have cooled off his hot reaction to her. By then, he hoped to know how the hell he was going to handle this problem that Sharon Fontaine had turned into. Big problem. Because despite the fact that she didn't like him, and that she was hell-bent on destroying his good name, he had been stupidly, ridiculously bowled over by Sharon. He couldn't remember when he'd desired a woman more.

Safely outside her apartment house, he stared up at the third floor. Why did he have to be attracted to her? Why a woman who was Scrooge to his Santa Claus? Could it be that he sensed that she was like he'd been once? Working too damned hard, hoping that he would never have time to think about or discover why he was so dissatisfied with life?

Okay, so he was beginning to understand the woman, Nick thought. What he didn't understand, though, was why he was feeling an inner pull toward a female who was hell-bent on taking all the fun out of *his* life. Life made no damned sense.

Not only was he going to have to get her off his back, he was now going to wash her out of his skin.

5

The next morning, Sharon had just finished speaking with her friend Catherine, filling her in on Peabody, when the phone on her desk at the *Tribune* rang again.

"This is Mr. Peabody. I—"

"Peabody, how are you?" she said, lowering her voice and covering the mouthpiece with her hand so she could speak as seductively as possible. "I dreamed about you—"

"Now cut that out!" Peabody exploded on the other end of the line. "Cut that out. You're frightening me. Yes, you are. And that's Mr. Peabody to you. Remember. *Mister* Peabody."

Mr. Bonacotti, don't you mean? Sharon thought. But, continuing in her plan to drive Bonacotti into confessing, she said sweetly, "Yes, darling." There was silence on the other end, but not for one minute did Sharon believe he'd hang up on her. She had the advantage here, and she knew it. Bonacotti needed to string her along. He had his own agenda—convincing her he was a do-gooder. At the risk of losing face in the community through her unfavorable articles, he wouldn't give up until she believed. As for her own agenda, well, she wasn't sure it was still entirely just getting a scoop on Saint Nick, even though she thought she was probably headed for disaster thinking that way.

"I don't like to be teased," Peabody said. "Not funny."

"I'm sorry." Sharon would have laughed, but she was starting to believe the Christmas celebration truly meant a lot to Nick Bonacotti. Not many men would carry out this charade to the point of letting their hair freeze outside. She'd actually felt flakes of ice on his head when she was drying his hair the night before. He seriously wanted to change her mind about him.

"Another meeting is arranged for Saturday," Peabody said to her. "Two o'clock. Can you make it to the newspaper? Pick you up there."

"Certainly, Mr. Peabody."

"Thank you. Farewell."

Well, that certainly sounded final. Sharon frowned as she hung up her phone. Perhaps she'd pushed the Saint a little too far last night, but she couldn't help herself. It had been safe, and somewhat titillating, playing a seductive game with Peabody, because she had figured, quite rightly, that he would run before he would respond outright. The fact that she might secretly have wished for a different response from him— from Nick Bonacotti—didn't matter. It was a game they were playing with each other. Just a game, nothing more. To wish for anything else was just foolish thinking. The important thing was getting the story she needed in order to stand out from the crowd of reporters and heat up her career. Nick Bonacotti, no matter how handsome and intriguing, was not going to stand in her way.

As Sharon paced the lobby of the *Tribune* on Saturday, she wished Saint Nick in person was going to show up, instead of Mr. Peabody. Not that she didn't like Peabody's personality, it was just that she would like to get to know the real version of the man. For her scoop, of course.

She blinked at the large, gold, sunburst clock on the wall and grimaced at the song skipping cheerily through the air, courtesy of piped music. If she heard "I Saw Mommy Kissing Santa Claus" one more time, she was personally going to rip out the wires to the speakers herself. If this got any worse, she was going to have to start wearing her earplugs permanently—

"Oh, look!" The receptionist caught her arm and pointed toward the door. "Santa Claus!"

"Sharon?" the large figure of Santa called as he came through the door, white beard and all. She recognized him from the Extravaganza. "Are you ready?"

"He's here for you?" the receptionist squealed. "Oh, how delicious! Wait till I tell everybody. Disaster date number two!"

With a harsh sound of exasperation, Sharon slipped a bill out of her wallet, opened the receptionist's fingers, and pushed it into her hand with a meaningful look. The receptionist covered her eyes with the palm of her hand.

Sharon shot toward Santa with another groan in her throat. Peabody was getting his revenge on her and he probably didn't even know it. She would be broke if this kept up.

She walked in front of Santa toward the door. "Where's Peabody?"

"He said he didn't feel well. Something about getting overheated a few days ago."

Her lips parted in a smirk. So, she had affected him, after all. "Are we going in your van?" she asked, remembering the vehicle with the sunshine yellow flowers from the night of the Extravaganza. She hitched her purse up over her shoulder and walked outside with him.

"We almost have to," Santa told her. "We have presents to deliver."

"Oh. Great."

Santa's blue eyes challenged her less-than-enthusiastic response. "You don't want to help me give out toys at the community center?"

She shrugged. If she had to, to get a story, she would. But she wasn't going to attempt to explain her dislike of Christmas to a man playing Santa Claus.

Once in the front seat, she was able to see the four huge white sacks filling the rear, stuffed with round objects.

"Let me guess," she said, pointing her thumb backward at the sacks. "Courtesy of Saint Nick?"

Santa started up the van and glanced at her from behind his wire-rimmed glasses. "Why are you so against Saint Nick's making others happy?"

"I'm not against it, exactly. I just think there has to be more to it. I'm a reporter. We're paid to examine motives, get to the bottoms of stories. If Saint Nick has some scheme in mind, the public should be warned."

"Then if you discover Saint Nick really is a saint, you'll print that, too?" He pulled out into the street.

She hesitated a minute. "We already did a human interest story on Wheaton's self-proclaimed Santa Claus—no offense—"

"None taken."

"So, no, we wouldn't do another feature. Perhaps a follow-up." But her editor's words echoed in her mind, almost as if Harley were sitting next to her, saying them again. *If I let you stir up the public, Fontaine, make sure you bring me something good. I don't want a reporter on this staff that the public is laughing at.* No, Nick Bonacotti *couldn't* be a saint. Her career was depending on it. Still, if he were, wouldn't that have to change her way of looking at life? At wishes? At dreams? At the very meaning of love?

No, Nick Bonacotti couldn't be a saint. She didn't want to delve that deeply into herself.

"So, Santa, why did you run away from me after the Extravaganza?" Staring at the man in the red velvet Santa suit, black belt and heavy white beard, it was kind of hard to remember he wasn't for real. But he wasn't. There was no Santa Claus.

"Mrs. Claus is very jealous." He chuckled, and then jerked the steering wheel to turn a corner.

She grabbed the dashboard. "Who pays you to work at the Extravaganza?"

"No one." His eyes widened in surprise and hurt, and he stared at her, a bit too long considering he was driving.

"Santa, the road."

"Oh," he said, turning his attention back to his driving. "Actually, I play Santa for the sheer fun of it."

Holding on to the dash, Sharon slumped against the cold leather of the seat. He was being as close-mouthed as Peabody, and she was going to have to work for every word of this article.

She'd never had occasion to visit the town's community center, so she didn't know what exactly went on there. Santa filled her in as they walked up to the huge brick building in the oldest section of town. Purple graffiti naming two popular gangs was sprayed on the front, ugly against the orange brick, and she shook her head as she pointed at it. "Things aren't getting any better in Wheaton since Saint Nick arrived, are they?"

"There are good people in this world—"

"I've heard this lecture, Santa," she said, thinking of Donnya Farmer at the day care.

"There are good people in this world," he repeated, "like Saint Nick, who believe in the ripple principle of love."

Her nose wrinkling as she tried to recall if she'd ever heard of what he was talking about before, Sharon opened the glass door for the elderly man. "Okay, Santa, I give up. What's the 'ripple principle of love'?"

"Different people call it different things, but basically..." Pausing, he looked around the bustling waiting room with its linoleum floor and rows of yellow, fuchsia, and gray-blue plastic chairs, and headed toward the reception counter. "Basically, Ms. Fontaine, it goes something like this—one person does something good for a stranger, who then goes on to help others, who then go on to help others. Like when you throw a rock in a pond. It only hits one spot, but the water ripples out to affect the whole pond. One person showing love and caring to another can impact a whole load of people."

She tapped his arm, and he turned to look at her.

"Lots of people give love," she said quietly. "Lots of people care. So why is the world whirling out of control? Why are so many people unhappy?"

"Because too many people expect something in return, and when they don't get it, they stop giving. With lots of people, a donation, a friendly word to another, or lending a helping hand comes once or twice at Christmas and then the spirit leaves them. They aren't rewarded, so they hide in their shells until the next Christmas, when they might give from their hearts again, if the spirit moves them. So often, it doesn't." His look was stern, as though she were one of the people he was referring to. "Do you know what I mean?"

Sharon's heart felt like a rubber ball being squeezed by an iron vise. He was describing what had happened to her after her mother's death, so many Christmases ago. The "spirit" of Christmas, as he called it, had left her and never returned. With it had gone her ability to reach out to others for anything. Especially love.

"If more people were like Saint Nick," Santa continued, not waiting for her answer, "spreading love all year round, we might just have enough rocks to really flood the pond.''

Before Sharon responded, a black-haired woman clad in a slim jean skirt, oversize pink sweater, and running shoes, called from down the hall. "Reverend Dunlevy!"

A minister, Sharon thought. Somehow, it didn't surprise her in the least, but she shook her head in mock disapproval at him for not mentioning it before. "So you really aren't Santa Claus."

"Would you be willing to bet your bottom dollar on that?" Reverend Dunlevy said, a twinkle in his eyes.

"He's better than Santa," the black-haired woman said, joining them. Sharon picked up a trace of a Spanish accent in her voice. "This center couldn't help half the people it does without Reverend Dunlevy."

Santa took her hand in his pudgy pink ones. "That's Santa to you, Marisa!"

The woman giggled. "You've finally come!"

"Along with a helper. This is Sharon Fontaine. Sharon, Marisa. She holds down the fort here."

"I'm pleased to meet you, Sharon," Marisa said. "So kind of you to drag the reverend away from the church for ten minutes."

"It wasn't hard," Sharon quipped. "In fact, I would say he was quite eager to show me what I've been missing."

Marisa frowned as though she didn't quite understand, but quickly recovered and directed them down the hall. "Well, I'm glad you're here. The kids will be ecstatic."

By the end of a half hour, Sharon had discovered that this gift recipient, a veteran who'd received a wheelchair-equipped van so he could drive himself places, was as effusive in his praise for Saint Nick as Donnya Farmer had been. If it weren't for Saint Nick getting him that van, Jerry March was certain he'd still be in his parents' home in a deep depression. Being able to get around meant he could come down here to the center, where he had gotten a job organizing recreation for vets. Today was their day to teach basketball to kids with mental handicaps.

"Thanks to Saint Nick, now we can all practice playing at home!" Jerry shouted exuberantly to the kids and veterans sitting on the gym floor, except for two, like him, who were in wheelchairs. Everyone clapped as Santa entered the gym with a couple of the center's workers carrying the sacks from the back of his van. They pulled open the drawstrings, and basketballs rolled out all over the place, at least twenty of them, going in every direction.

The kids watched, wide-eyed, while the vets, most in their forties, hid smiles and wiped at their gleaming, teary eyes. At first, overwhelmed by the balls bouncing and rolling around them, no one moved, but then a girl with Down syndrome scurried after one of the balls, threw it up in the air and caught it, laughing. Less than three seconds later, everyone got into the act. Sharon pushed a strand of hair out of her eyes as she watched and thought about Nick Bonacotti.

He ought to be there. She'd like to see how he would have reacted to all this happiness. Would there be a mist in his eyes, similar to the one in her own, watching these children? Would he understand how much this meant to all the people in this gym? If he really cared about these people, why hadn't he come himself?

Torn, she pulled in a deep, trembling breath. Was she wrong about Nick Bonacotti? She suddenly wanted to believe a man who had brought this much happiness to these kids and veterans had no selfish motives. But in the bottom of her thoughts, the question still remained. If she were wrong about him, why wouldn't he talk about Tracy Rhodes?

"So, have you changed your mind about Saint Nick?" Santa asked from behind her.

"I'll admit I'm impressed," she said slowly, truthfully. "Those kids were really tickled. So were the vets. Saint Nick's doing a lot of good in Wheaton."

"Then you won't be writing any more editorials about him."

She didn't want to lie or give this man playing Santa any caustic answers—after all, he was a minister, and she'd been raised to respect the church. But neither did she want to tell Reverend Dunlevy the truth, that she'd started something with her editorial against Saint Nick she now would have to finish, or she wouldn't have a career. The idea that her one big attempt at breaking into the big time might be a grievous error in judgment frightened her. She couldn't be wrong about Nick.

She just couldn't. But what if she was?

The image of Nick sitting in her kitchen appeared in her mind, and without wanting to, she remembered the feel of the smooth skin, and the warmth of his chest when she'd reached down to unbutton his shirt. She heard his breathing once again, quickening as she touched him. Drawing in an enormous breath, she considered it all, and realized Nick appealed to her on all levels.

Physically, definitely. But he also appealed to her because—no matter what his motive was—he was the one responsible for all these smiling faces in front of her now. Nick was the Santa Claus she'd prayed would come into her life for at least half her teenaged years, but never had. The thought that he was here now, when she least wanted him, confused her, so very much.

One of the children ran to them to hug Santa, and when he was gone, Reverend Dunlevy prompted, "Sharon? Will you be writing more editorials about him?"

"Why won't Saint Nick tell everyone why he's doing this?" she asked, staring earnestly at the other man. "If he gave me an interview, he could explain his motivation for playing Santa. It might have that— what did you call it, ripple effect?—that spurs others to give to others, too. I could keep his identity a secret."

"I'll relay your message to Mr. Peabody that you would like an interview. I'm sure he'll tell Saint Nick."

Sharon ignored his obvious irritation. He sounded as though he really believed the two were different men. If Nick Bonacotti was the saint everyone thought he was, why couldn't he trust a minister enough to keep his secret? Could it be that the minister would have reason not to like him if he knew who Saint Nick really was? She was becoming so frustrated over this! Every time she wanted to believe in Nick, a reason popped up why she shouldn't.

"Do you truly want to help others with this article, Sharon?" the reverend asked suddenly.

She answered automatically. "Of course. The paper does human interest articles all the time to inspire people—"

"But do *you* really want to help others by writing an article about Saint Nick and why he does what he does?"

"I'm not pretending to be the saint here," she said a little defensively.

"Then consider this," he continued. "Unless an interview like that comes from your heart, it isn't going to inspire anyone to give anything. You won't find the right words, the right message."

She started to answer and then stopped, staring at him. Her motivation for this article was success, pure and simple. Dunlevy was as much as saying that was bad. But was it really? She wasn't sure she could write from the heart, not about Christmas. She wasn't sure how much heart she had left at her ripe old age of twenty-five.

Life had pretty much stolen all her heart away from her, starting before she'd been born when her father hadn't cared enough to stick around to marry her mother, to the point where the Christmas angel hadn't cared enough about her to grant her wish to keep her mother alive. She was sorry, but that was the way she was. The world was survival of the fittest. To her, staying cynical meant she wouldn't expect anything from anyone. It also meant she didn't have to hurt when people failed her.

"I don't think you're being entirely realistic, Reverend. My motivation in writing this article is that I have to earn a living and keep my job, while reporting the truth. That has to be my first priority."

Reverend Dunlevy shook his head slightly, rustling his beard against his velvet suit. "I can't change your way of thinking, but please keep in mind some things in life are not meant to be interfered with, such as people with hearts like Saint Nick. He gives without asking for anything in return, out of love for fellow human beings. If you try to bring him down, you might find yourself regretting it. You may ruin a good man."

Reverend Dunlevy's words were still in her mind the next evening as Sharon lingered behind the fire door on the second floor of Bonacotti Industries, watching the cleaning staff walking onto the elevator for their nine o'clock break. The minister's philosophy of life sounded pretty, but it wasn't realistic, not when you had to survive in a dog-eat-dog world. If she didn't get a story, she'd be in hot water with Harley and could ruin her career. Since she wouldn't ask Catherine for help, unlike Nick Bonacotti, she couldn't afford to be a saint.

Which was why she had decided it was time to sneak into Bonacotti Industries. She was going to get the written proof she needed that Nick was *Saint* Nick, and then she could confront him with her questions.

He'd be forced to answer, or risk his identity being exposed. Her plan seemed foolproof.

Once the hallway was clear, Sharon opened the door and darted down the hall, smoothing the starched pink uniform she wore with one hand and carrying a green feather duster with the other. On her pocket was sewn the name Irma. Covering her brown hair was a wiry black wig, and perched on her nose were the huge tortoise-rimmed reading glasses she'd purchased off the rack in the pharmacy section of the supermarket. They made everything appear huge, and she felt a little off center as she tested Nick Bonacotti's office door. Since the staff supposedly came back after their break, she had figured they wouldn't have bothered to lock the door. She was right. It was open.

Seconds later, adrenaline surging through her, she searched the file cabinet in Nick Bonacotti's private office. He had to have some sort of correspondence about what he was doing, maybe receipts for income tax purposes. But somehow, she would bet there was more—like an invitation list for the Extravaganza.

She glanced at her rhinestone watch. Twelve minutes left to find her proof and Tracy Rhodes's whereabouts. If she got lucky, she could pop two stories at once.

In a file titled Recipients, she found two good letters and was just about to take them to the copy machine in the outer office when she heard a door opening.

''Damn!'' she whispered, jamming the letters back into the file and sliding the file drawer closed as noiselessly as possible. Scooping up her feather duster, she headed toward the door and pulled it open.

Nick Bonacotti stood there.

"Whoops!" she said, stooping her back and bowing her head so he couldn't see her face. Her nerves sizzled and her body heated treacherously as she caught the faint scent of his cologne. "I'ma all done ina here," she said, the accent the best she could do on the spur of the moment. She waved her feather duster at him. "Got to take'a my break."

Since Nick continued to block her way, she brushed his emerald green cotton shirt with her feather duster. Startled, he stepped back once, and she peeked at him over her glasses.

Up close, without the Peabody getup, he was striking, with a rugged jawline she ached to touch. His eyebrows weren't growing together anymore, and she realized he must have pasted on fake ones to play Peabody. The sexy smell of his cologne made her recall that this man had been the same one who had kissed her before, and how electrifying that kiss had been. No matter that he'd been a nerd then. He was heavenly now.

A splatter of heat sizzled through her. Saint Nick in the flesh was every bit as overwhelming as Saint Nick the legend. But she didn't want to think about that. She didn't need to get her heart involved in this story. The fact remained—legally, she was trespassing. Among other things. She had to get out of there.

"You gonna to'a move outta my way?" she asked. "I gotta work to do."

"Who are you?"

"Irma. Froma the temp agency." She kept her head bent and her back hunched. She could see him, but she couldn't read the stiffened muscles of his facial expression. Was he angry?

"You gonna move," she asked, "or am I gonna hafta worry?" She had all the confidence in the world that he would let her go. What choice did he have, except to call the police? He didn't need that kind of publicity.

He smiled and stepped into the office, closing the door behind him. "Maybe you'll have to worry."

"W-what?" she squeaked, stepping backward, brandishing the feather duster like a weapon. "I'ma worker here. I gotta—"

"What's your name?"

Shaken as she was, it took Sharon a second to recall the name she'd embroidered on her pocket. "Irma," she said. "Yes, Irma."

"Well, Irma, since the rest of the staff goes on break together, I can only assume you stayed behind for a reason."

"To clean," she said as he took another step toward her and she backed up. "Uh, Mr. Bonacotti, I really have to be going."

Oops, she'd forgotten her accent.

He grinned.

"You sure you didn't stick around because you wanted to get to know me better?" he asked, stepping closer.

"Hardly," she said under her breath, running to the far side of his desk. Lifting up the feather duster, she punctuated her words with it. "You better letta me go,

Mr. Bonacotti. What woulda your sainted Italian mother say'a about this?''

"She's been after me to bring home an Italian wife," Nick said. "Care to audition?"

"I'm not available," she snapped. "Do you always accost the help?"

"Only the pretty ones." Swiftly rounding the desk, he caught her just as she cleared the side, slipping one arm around her middle and lifting her off her feet.

"Let me go!" she said. He was as strong as she'd envisioned. Stronger even. Right now, her feet kicking in the air, she felt like he was Superman.

"I'll make you a deal," he said. "You give me a kiss, and I won't call the police."

She stopped kicking.

"I thought that might get you." He chuckled as he put her down on her feet.

Rearranging her pink uniform, Sharon tried to remember to keep her back stooped, tried to remember she was Irma, the cleaning woman. But as his large hands settled on her shoulders and turned her, and as he slipped his fingers under her chin and lifted her head to look at him, all she could think of was that she was going to kiss a man who'd made her heart throb and her knees weak, even when he'd been dressed as a nerd.

She barely noticed when he took her glasses off and slipped them into her uniform pocket, just before he shut his eyes and she shut hers. She did notice the heat of his lips on her cheek, and the sensual way his mouth traced a path down to her lips....

The feather duster slipped from her fingers, and she reached upward to encircle his neck. The kiss seemed so right, so natural, so breathtakingly good, that she wanted it to go on forever. It wasn't just the tenderness of his kiss, it was the strength of his arms around her waist, the woodsy scent of him, the minty taste of him. The man of her dreams had her in his arms and wasn't letting her go. It was all she could want for Christmas, for forever.

His arms remaining around her waist, he pulled back from her and smiled his now familiar Peabody smile.

There was something in his smile.... She gazed at him, wondering if he was feeling the same thing she was. Like there was some depth to the kiss that had nothing to do with sexual attraction.

No, she was kidding herself. Nick Bonacotti was a saint, and she didn't believe in Christmas. If she let herself start feeling anything for him, she'd only be sorry later. They lived by two differing philosophies, and she found his a bit naive. There couldn't be anything between them except sexual attraction, and that would be impossible to handle, once she wrote her exposé. She wasn't a big enough fool to believe that even love could survive what she needed to do to Nick—not that she was in love or anything.

"So tell me, Sharon," he drawled, pulling her from her thoughts, "what did you discover in my files?"

6

"The glasses," Sharon whispered, touching her unadorned, peach-tinted cheekbones. Considering Nick had seen through her disguise immediately, he thought her shock at being discovered was almost funny.

He realized he was still holding her, mostly because in his arms she responded like less of a cynical reporter and more like a woman—and women he could deal with, thanks to growing up in a family of them. In a way, handling Sharon and seeing if he could crack through her cynical reporter shell was becoming a diversion from his work as fun, interesting, and necessary as playing Saint Nick was to him. Fun because he got to kiss her, interesting because he wondered why Sharon was the only person in Wheaton who wasn't in awe of Saint Nick, and necessary because he wasn't about to let her change his life.

She smiled weakly. "I guess I should have tried a blond wig."

"Wouldn't have done any good," he said, letting go of her. "You were kind of hard to miss, even under those glasses. Your accent was straight out of a low-budget horror flick."

"So I'm no actress."

"You aren't much of a reporter, either, not if you have to resort to trespassing to get your stories. I take it you were snooping?" He swept his hand toward the file cabinet.

She didn't answer. Instead she pulled off her wig and laid it on his desk. Removing some hairpins, she shook her head, letting her wavy, dark brown hair curve around her shoulders in dancing waves. The brown flecks in her green eyes reflected the glow of the lamp he'd kept lit on his desk. Nick knew this because he couldn't take his eyes off her.

"You're Saint Nick," she said.

"Am I?" he asked, his voice noncommittal as he crossed his arms over his chest. Her defiant eyes never wavered from his. Nick couldn't tell what she was really thinking; she was such a treasure trove of contradictions. She'd reacted to his kiss in a heartfelt, helpless-to-resist way he would swear was not an act, yet she was after her story and therefore could not be trusted. She'd broken into his office, yet she was acting as though she had every right to question him.

Damn it all, anyway. This one little lady had him stumped.

Maybe it was his own fault. He'd been fantasizing about her since she'd run her fingers through his hair—no, who was he kidding? He'd been dreaming of her since he'd first come face-to-face with her. He had to get his control back.

"What makes you think I'm Wheaton's mystery man?" he asked, walking to his chair. Sitting down behind his desk, he propped his feet up and interlaced his fingers behind his head as though he hadn't a care in the world.

"Don't bother to deny it. You're not talking to some awestruck Wheatonian."

"You sure about that?" he said, shooting her his grin again. "You seemed pretty awestruck when I kissed you."

The sexy, cynical reporter actually blushed bright red. Nick couldn't believe it. Suddenly he wondered if she were less worldly, less in control, than she was pretending.

Her chin tilted up defiantly. "You're also Mr. Peabody."

"Am I?" He smiled again. "You're so certain?"

"I kissed you both." Her lips came together as if to say, *beat that*.

"Is that what you're going to use when you write your next article on Saint Nick? I can see it now." He lowered his voice to mimic a television newscaster's. " 'Having kissed both Nick Bonacotti and Mr. Peabody, this reporter can safely testify to the fact they are one and the same man.' Tell me, Miss Fontaine, is comparing kisses like wine tasting? Do you have to practice a lot?"

"I followed you after we went to Donnya Farmer's, and saw you come out of the men's room," she said, irritated. "When I investigated, I found Peabody's clothes in sacks in the utility closet."

"Oh. I see." That certainly explained her performance a couple nights ago with the blow-dryer. She had known who he was and had been out to fluster him, to get the upper hand. He had to admit, she'd almost succeeded. "So then you decided to come here and get the paperwork to prove I'm Saint Nick."

"How do you know I haven't already gotten some of the evidence I needed on another night? You should lock your files, Mr. Bonacotti."

"I work in the evenings," he said, cocking his eyebrow. "It's inconvenient to worry about locking the files every time I leave the office." Letting his feet fall back to the floor, he leaned forward in his chair and picked up her wiry black wig, popping a couple of the springy curls with his fingers. "You're bluffing, Miss Fontaine."

Her eyes were suddenly sharp and focused, and she was every bit the reporter. "You sent a letter to your sister saying you contacted Donnya Farmer about getting her present and signed the invitation Saint Nick."

"You print that, I'll have you nailed for trespassing."

"Maybe, maybe not. What do you say, Nick? Will you tell me why you started this Saint Nick thing?"

He tossed her wig back onto the desk. She certainly was cool. But he'd realized that when he'd read her editorial about Saint Nick. He'd wanted to warm her up to his way of thinking, but if seeing Donnya and Jerry hadn't given her the Christmas spirit, nothing ever would. This was one lady he wasn't sure if love could change. She wasn't going to leave him alone until he gave her an interview.

He sighed in resignation. "I want your handwritten agreement that whatever you write concerning Saint Nick, you won't identify me."

"No problem," Sharon said, whipping a small notebook from her apron pocket and pulling a pen from the monogrammed holder on his desk. A couple minutes later he had the signed and dated document in his hands. Sticking it in his desk, he locked the drawer and pocketed the key.

She watched his every move, especially the last one.

"Don't get any ideas," he warned. "My pockets are deeper than Peabody's."

She rolled her eyes. Seeing that he looked ready for the interview, she perched on the edge of a chair with her notebook.

Nick's eyes went right to her crossed legs encased in nylons, and he shifted in his chair. Why the hell did Sharon Fontaine have to be so damned appealing?

"Hurry up," he half growled. The sooner he had her out of his life, the better.

"Why do you have to hide your identity?"

He held up her wig. "With the trouble *you've* gone to, just to get to me, you really have to ask? Multiply your efforts by the eighty or so thousand in this city and you've got your answer. I'd have people trying all sorts of schemes like this one, or lined up from here to the *Tribune* waiting to get a piece of the rock. I don't have enough money for that, or enough patience."

Abashed, she stiffened, and then furiously shook her head. "I'm hardly on the same level as the rest of the community. I didn't ask Saint Nick for anything you'd pay money for."

His eyes glittered. "No, you just wanted a story."

"I was referring to the night of the Extravaganza."

"Oh, yes. Your impossible wish for a man."

Was she so unappealing? Bending over her note-book and scribbling, Sharon hoped Nick couldn't see the hurt in her eyes. *What about you, Nick?* a small voice inside her asked. *You kissed me. Twice.*

Nick Bonacotti, the man of her dreams? At the same time the small voice piped up, *Forget it!* her brain was asking, *why not him?* Yes, she needed to find out what made Nick Bonacotti the man he was so she would know why he *couldn't* be the man of her dreams.

She glanced up at Nick. His inky blue eyes were centered on her. "I also need to know what drives you to give away your hard-earned money. Do you feel guilty about something? Is it a tax write-off? Are you paying back society for some evil?"

"I'm a nice guy."

"Seriously."

His eyes pinned Sharon. "Seriously."

"Mr. Bonacotti, I am not going to write that you give away thousands each Christmas because you're a nice guy. Was there some incident in your childhood where you did something wrong, or something like that, and now you're making up for it, maybe? Think. There has to be some deep-rooted psychological reason why you do this."

"Life has really jerked you around, hasn't it?"

The pain flitted across her face for a glimmer of an instant, leaving behind a look of confusion, and something pulled at Nick's heart. Sharon *had* been hurt. "What are you talking about?" she asked.

Nick didn't pursue it. "Contrary to popular belief nowadays, Miss Fontaine, some people actually are normal, and from very functional families." Standing, he walked over to lean back against his desk, wanting to unnerve her with his closeness and get her to talk to him. From the way she stiffened, her luminous eyes widening, he knew his move had done the trick. She was now off-guard.

"I didn't have a traumatic childhood, Sharon. I didn't get into any mischief that wouldn't be considered boyhood pranks—"

"Such as?"

"About the worst thing that ever happened to me was that the police brought me home when I was nine for climbing on the roof of the downtown bank with a friend of mine."

Sharon's smile lit up her face. "They thought you were going to rob the bank?"

He shook his head. "They thought we were going to jump off the top onto the sidewalk."

"Of course, they were wrong."

He grinned. "Actually, they were right. My sister squealed on us. We were going to see who could do it without breaking anything."

"Oh, my gosh."

"We were only nine," he said defensively.

"Your mother had her hands full with you."

"Her fondest saying was, 'Nickolo, you are such a boy!'"

Her laughter pealed through the room. Nick smiled back and shifted his weight onto his other foot. Relaxing, her attention caught by the movement of his legs, Sharon eyed his jeans, the way they hugged his hips and outlined the muscles of his thighs. With great difficulty, she returned her concentration to what he was saying.

"When I was around eleven, I had an after-school job sweeping my uncle's barbershop, and in the slow times, he taught me how to whittle. He'd carve small, intricate, dump trucks with real wheels, wheel barrels, that sort of thing. One Christmas, he gave them away as presents to the little kids going by the shop, just to make them happy."

Sharon could almost see the boy he must have been, a happy-go-lucky, as-the-spirit-moved-him type of kid, with two parents who loved him. Lucky him.

"I never forgot the looks on those kids' faces when they got those toys," Nick said. "So a couple of years ago, when I was bored, I decided to put some life back into Wheaton."

"After this factory made you rich, you mean."

"No." He leaned forward on the desk. "I had a trust fund which I parlayed into a hefty amount. But I am by no means rich." The trust fund had been, in reality, from an insurance policy cashed in when his father died, but that was no one's business. He just had always thought his father would approve of what he was doing with the money. "Believe me, if the gift recipients asked for the moon, I wouldn't be able to give it to them."

"But you put 'money is no object' on the invitations."

"I know. Doesn't it renew your faith in human beings, Sharon, that no one has yet asked for something that I couldn't comfortably get for them? Remarkable, huh?" No one, that was, until Sharon, he thought. He wondered why he didn't just tell her of course he couldn't get her someone who would love her forever. But then he flashed on the wistfulness that had been in her voice when she'd asked for a man that night, and he knew he somehow had to help Sharon to be a little happier in life. He would do no less for anyone he felt compassion for, he told himself. And besides, what the heck—it *was* Christmas.

Sitting in silence, Sharon thought about what he'd said. "Maybe it was remarkable, or maybe you chose people who were so poor anything looks like a step up to them."

He sighed. "What makes you so cynical?"

"*I'm* interviewing *you*. So why did you invite me to receive a gift? You know I'm a reporter. You had to know I was just waiting for something like an invitation so I could get more information on you."

He began to pace. For the first time he actually seemed disturbed. "Nobody was ever negative toward Saint Nick before."

She'd hurt his feelings, Sharon realized.

"I wanted to convince you that I was sincere about making people happy. I thought after you talked to Jerry and Donnya you'd believe there was nothing else to this. I know what you told Reverend Dunlevy, but have you changed your mind since then about me?"

Sharon didn't know what to say. The concern in those gorgeous eyes of his was evident. He wanted her to believe. He truly did. Maybe if she tried to explain her side . . .

"Look, I could see that your gifts made a difference in Jerry's and Donnya's lives." She clicked her pen and stuck it behind her ear. "For now. But what happens if the center closes and Jerry loses his job and can't get another because he isn't qualified? Wouldn't it have been better to spend that money on retraining him?"

"I can see your point. What field would you suggest? Anything you name could have funding cuts and throw Jerry out on the streets. Not even a government job is a sure thing anymore." Leaning down, he grabbed the thin arms of her chair. Sharon gulped again as her eyes flew to meet his.

"Jerry and Donnya love what they're doing," he said gently. "Why can't you just take things at face value?"

Sharon's breath caught. Any minute he might start asking her other questions. He might want to start getting close to her, and she wasn't ready. She didn't believe in Nick. She couldn't.

Pushing him out of her way, she stood. "The gifts you're giving seem newsworthy and flamboyant and not a real solution to anyone's problems. I asked Saint Nick for a husband to point that out to you, but apparently your ability to understand isn't any better than mine."

"I don't believe you," he said incredulously. For a second he'd seen vulnerability on her delicate features. He thought he'd finally reached her.

"You said you aren't wealthy," she continued. "I think your ultimate aim in being Saint Nick is to get publicity for your business that is worthy of CNN coverage. I also think you invited me to get a gift because you wanted to use me and the *Tribune* to get started on that publicity campaign."

He shook his head in disgust, but Sharon saw a chance to rile him into the truth, and she wasn't letting go. "If you were found out, you could even claim I started the whole publicity ball rolling with the article you knew I would write. Your nice, unblemished image would stay that way.

"Everyone has an angle these days, Mr. Bonacotti. Isn't yours really to get nationwide publicity for your toy business? Spend a moderate amount to gain millions?"

"All that effort taking you to meet Donnya and Jerry—that was for nothing, wasn't it? You didn't learn a thing about me." He watched her lips go tightly together, and her eyes flash, and he softened his tone. "What made you this way, Sharon? So skeptical? So disbelieving?"

That whiskey-smooth, caring tone had returned, and Sharon wanted to believe he cared. Truly cared and really wanted to know why she didn't believe in Santa Claus, or in the love he was so freely giving away.

"Sharon? Tell me. Maybe I can help."

Glassy warm tears began to fall down her cheeks, and she turned around to leave, horrified that she was breaking down in front of this man she barely knew. She hadn't shed a tear for anyone, or anything, since her mother died.

A renewed surge of wild grief that she hadn't believed in the Christmas angel enough to save her mother bolted through her, and it made her angry.

Why couldn't she accept that no amount of faith would have saved her mother? God, she hated Christmas. The holiday only reminded her of how little she had in her life. And she hated Nick Bonacotti for dredging all this up for her again.

"I'm leaving."

"This interview isn't over," Nick said, catching her arm to stop her from flying toward the door.

Her green eyes flashed furious fire at being stopped. "Saint Nick isn't for real," she snapped. "He can't be. Gifts don't just come raining down from heaven, or from anywhere else at Christmas, or any other time. Wishes aren't granted magically. There are no Christmas miracles!"

"That's not true," he argued.

"Yes, it is!" Her chest trembled as she drew a deep breath, struggling to control both her anger and her crying. "I prayed to the Christmas angel my mother swore held the spirit of Christmas. Over and over I prayed, believing it would make a difference." She raised her eyes and stared at him. "But it didn't."

He let go of her arm, and she stood, glaring at him.

"What was supposed to have happened, Sharon?"

"It doesn't matter." She shook her head and shoved her notebook into her pocket, letting the hair cascading down either side of her face block her view of him. "The world is a hard place, and it isn't getting any better. You're making people in Wheaton believe in magic, and it's just plain wrong to do that. Can't you see? You're doing no one any good by teaching them to believe in miracles, not if they look to someone else—or worse, some magical spirit—to solve their problems."

Nick found himself reaching out to cup her shoulder with one hand and tilting her chin up with the fingers of the other so that she had to look him in the eye. He needed to know why she was like this. He suddenly wanted to help her more than anything else in the world right then. "Sharon, what was supposed to have happened?"

She tried to shake him off. He held her gently but firmly in place with both hands. "Tell me, Sharon."

"My mother was supposed to have lived. The cancer killed her anyway." The words came out in a rush of pain and more tears, and she tried to pull away to leave. Nick wrapped both his arms around her and held her against him until she quit fighting and settled into his strength.

"You haven't been able to lean on anyone in a long time, have you?" he asked quietly.

"There was Catherine, at work, but then she moved away. But I don't need anyone." She wiped at her eyes impatiently, then rested her cheek in the crook of his neck, trying to concentrate on the cologne he was wearing, on the velvetlike feel of his shirt—on anything except how much pain she was in. "I have my career."

"I said that once, too. But I was wrong."

"Well, you're the saint. I'd expect that." She straightened. Her eyes were wet and glittery, and tired.

He reached up and wiped away some stray tears. "You're all reporter again, aren't you?" he asked. "I think I liked Irma the Cleaning Lady better."

"And I preferred Mr. Peabody," she said crisply.

A slow grin split his lips. "I like you, toooo, Miss Scrooge." Mr. Peabody, nasal and whiny, was back. Sharon squeezed her eyes shut, trying hard to remember she was angry at Nick's stubbornness. Trying hard not to remember Peabody's—Nick's—kisses.

"I want a date, Shaaaron." Nick was asking her because he wanted to know exactly what Sharon was planning to write about him. Also, he wanted another crack at changing her and finding out if her cynicism was masking a very nice person worth knowing.

"No!" she said, whirling around and heading toward the door. If she stayed and Nick kept this up, she might laugh. If she laughed, she might give in.

"Why not? Don't you like me?" he asked. His voice ripped through her ears. "Shaaaron?"

"Yes, I like you."

"Then come on a date. You'll have fun. Yes, indeedy."

"Why?" she pleaded, wiping at her glistening eyes again and facing him. "I have to write an article about you. You know that. My career is at stake. You're going to end up hating me for it."

Nick shrugged, his eyes twinkling as he crossed his arms over his chest. "What reporter in her right mind would pass up a real chance to get to know the Saint better before the big exposé?"

Pulling in a deep breath, Sharon finally went against her better judgment. "All right. But no Peabody clothes."

"Aw, gee," he said. "Not even if I get a new hat to go with the suit?"

Throwing up her hands, she started to leave again.

"Sharon?"

"What?"

He handed her the feather duster. "You might have to return this to the newspaper's prop department."

"We don't have—" Too late, she realized he was teasing. "Goodbye, Nick." Turning away from him once more, she took a step.

"Sharon?"

"What!" she asked without turning to look at him.

"I'll call you about the date. My schedule's awfully heavy with the holidays. It may take a couple days."

"Okay." Knowing he couldn't see her face, she smiled. "Anything else?"

"Yes."

With a sigh, she turned and was swept into his arms. With breathless abandon, she didn't protest. All at once her senses spun, and then he claimed her lips in a deep kiss as he crushed her to him. The strength in his arms seeped into her as his mouth covered hers as hungrily as hers tasted his. Right now, she thought with an inward groan, she wanted Nick Bonacotti. In bed. Naked.

She tore herself away and said, breathily, "I'm still going to write the article."

Although his breathing was labored, too, he made every effort to look nonchalant. "Okay."

"I have no choice."

"Yes, you do. Life is just one long series of choices. We make decisions on what we think we need at the moment." He crossed his arms over his chest again. "So, Sharon, what do you need right now?"

She wet her lips and swallowed. It didn't help. "I need to get out of here." Hurrying from the room, she refused to look back.

Nick stared at the empty doorway for a long time. Sharon Fontaine could use some fun. Something to look forward to besides work. As exasperating as she was, she'd touched him with her tears, and he wanted to be that something that melted away the pain in her life. Why he was going to fool with a woman hell-bent on ruining him, he wasn't sure. He just knew he wouldn't be able to rest until she thought he was the greatest thing since... since...

Since Christmas.

7

When was Nick going to call? Did she really want him to? The words on the screen in front of Sharon blurred. Her fingers paused over the keys, then dropped down to rest on them. Almost four days had passed since she'd last seen Nick, and she couldn't get him out of her mind. She'd covered a mayor's press conference, a Christmas plea of a homeless family, and the opening of a new store. Through all of them, she kept reliving Nick's kiss and the way it had lit a flame inside her that burned hot clear to her toes. On the other hand, every time she thought of the way he'd caused her to blurt out her hurt over her mother's death, she dreaded Nick's calling.

No doubt about it, he had the ability to make her *feel*, and that made him dangerous to her. It was safer not to feel anything. It wouldn't hurt as much when Nick left her alone again.

"Fontaine, are you wearing those earplugs again?"

Jerking her head around, she stared guiltily at Harley, who had been running his fingers through his hair—something he did when frustrated. This time he'd ruffled his hair like a peacock's feathers at half-mast, which was a sign that things were especially tense. Wanting him to think she'd been concentrating on her work, she replied in a light voice, "Sorry. I was working on the store opening piece."

"Before you get back to that," he said, "how's the follow-up on Saint Nick coming?"

Recalling her cocksure attitude the day the invitation had arrived, she hesitated.

Harley noticed. "Don't tell me you don't have anything," he warned.

"I will have soon," she promised, her gaze flying to the phone, her mind willing it to ring. It didn't.

"You'd better. Before Christmas, when it will bring in the most readers. After Christmas it will be a moot point. Get on it." He took a breath.

Since his tone brooked no argument, Sharon didn't dare try to explain to him that she was afraid she might have a conflict of interest where Nick Bonacotti was concerned. She needed her job too much as a buffer against the loneliness in her life.

"I'll see what I can come up with, Harley," she promised dully. "Is that all?"

"No, I want you to go see what's going on down at the shelter on Clement Street with that homeless family. Somebody's called a press conference—"

"A press conference? The only press in town is us!" Sharon said.

Harley shrugged. "So go see. It's for noon. If you're the only one there, it won't matter if you're late."

It was eleven-fifty. Grimacing at Harley, she grabbed her coat, making a split decision to walk to the shelter because it would be quicker than waiting for her Toyota to warm up. But the wind was cold, and she muttered curses under her breath all the way.

If the paper paid better, she'd have a new car she could just hop into and drive.

If she only still hated Nick Bonacotti, she could write her story with no guilt.

If her only living relative hadn't gone and died on her, she wouldn't be alone in the world. Then she would never have been lonely enough to have the least little fantasy about Mr. Peabody in the first place, which had led, in the second place, to her ongoing fantasies about Nick Bonacotti.

"Sharon," she muttered under her breath, watching her words blow out frosty white in front of her nose, "you *are* losing it." Opening the door to the shelter, she hurried inside to the large community room, vowing, for one hour at least, not to think about Nick Bonacotti, or his alter ego, or Christmas itself, for that matter.

Which would be impossible to do, she saw the second she slipped through the door, which was bordered by gold garland. With only a week and a half until Christmas, someone had put up a tree in one corner, and it sparkled with tinsel and twinkling lights. A cutout of Santa Claus and reindeer stretched along one long wall for almost seven feet, and crocheted white snowflakes danced in rings hanging in front of the windows. The room brimmed with Christmas spirit and love.

Neither of which she had. She wiped away her emotions impatiently as she glanced to the front of the room.

What she'd said to Harley had been the truth—there *were* only two newspapers in town, a weekly and the *Tribune,* whose main competition came from the nearby Springfield paper. She saw two reporters from there, a television camera, the mayor of Wheaton, and no less than five other people she couldn't identify talking excitedly to one another.

"It's twelve now," John McFry, the director of Clement House, announced at the microphone. "Please take your seats. Press can remain up front in case there are questions."

When the podium cleared, she saw Nick Bonacotti in his Peabody disguise—so much for forgetting about him for any length of time. Today his tie and socks were the neon orange that hunters donned for the woods so people wouldn't mistake them for animals.

She snapped her mouth shut. What was Nick doing here? Every muscle in her body strained to go nearer to him, but she knew that would be a mistake.

Sliding into a seat, she waited as others did the same. She kept glancing at Nick—no, she'd better think of him as Peabody. He was here as Saint Nick's representative, and she wasn't going to blow his cover. Not until she figured out what she was going to do about him.

The low buzz of the audience didn't cease until John McFry held up his hands for quiet and stood in front of the microphones the television and radio people had set up. Expectantly, the crowd waited.

"We are here today because of Saint Nick."

People cheered. Pursing her lips, Sharon watched Nick. His blue eyes were warm and glowing behind his glasses as he surveyed the crowd. He was loving this, almost as though the admiration of the crowd fed him somehow—but not in a bad way. Lifting her note-book from her purse, she wrote the thought down. She had to take notes about this press meeting anyway, she defended herself inwardly. She might as well make the best of it.

"You may or may not know that our ability to fill all the rooms of this shelter depends on the month-to-month generosity of the citizens of Wheaton. Well, Saint Nick, through his representative, has gathered several people together to adopt this shelter for a year. They will make regular monthly donations into the shelter's general fund so that we don't have to rely on hit-and-miss contributions."

Clapping filled the room.

"Now, Mr. Peabody wants to say a few words. Due to the fact that Saint Nick once again wishes to re-main anonymous, Mr. Peabody will answer abso-lutely no questions afterward."

Peabody ambled over to the microphones and leaned down. "Uh, testing. One, five, eight, twelve— *boo!*" His voice boomed over the speakers and he stepped back, surprised. The children giggled as though he were a clown sent for their entertainment. Peabody twisted his mouth and wiggled his nose. The kids laughed again, and he grinned at them.

"Saint Nick challenges everyone who can hear this to do something goood for somebody else. Yes, he does. Kids—" he grinned again "—you can do this, tooo. Love somebody for no special reason."

His eyes found Sharon's. "There are a lot of people who need somebody, and maybe they don't even know it. Be good to them. Teach them there's a lot of love out there to be shared." Showing all his pearly teeth in a wide grin, he added, "Do it for Saint Nick."

Sharon's breath caught in her throat, and she flushed with pleasure. How did he manage to make her feel so good just by looking at her? It made no sense. Magnetism? How on earth was she going to do her story and keep her job?

The press began firing questions about Saint Nick, and who he was, and who the new benefactors of Clement House were, but Peabody ignored them and slipped through the door. John McFry stepped back up to the microphones and began answering some of the questions, but Sharon knew where the real story was. Shoving her notebook back into her purse, she rose and followed Nick.

Minutes later, she spotted him standing on the far side of an emerald green pickup. Her heels clicked on the sidewalk as she hurried toward him. "You never called."

"Uh-oh," Nick said in a perfect Peabody tone. "Watch it, Shaaaron, or I'll start thinking you missed me." He gave her his Peabody grin, and she smiled back, embarrassed because he was right. She had missed him. But she wasn't going to tell him that.

"I walked over," she said instead. "I didn't know you'd be here, but it's just as well you are. I wanted to talk to you. Can I have a ride back to the *Tribune?*" She pulled her coat collar more tightly around her neck.

"Sure. Hop in."

Once they were inside the pickup, he slipped his glasses off and into his pocket, and for all intents and purposes, became Nick Bonacotti—at least from the neck up. "Instead of my taking you back to work, how about that lunch date?"

She wanted to go, but some inner sense of self-preservation made her point to his suit. "In public?"

He grinned down at himself. "If you're worried about not fitting in with me, we could go to your place and you could put on your Irma outfit."

For a wild, crazy few seconds she pictured doing that, and her lips curved in a smile. "We'd be quite a team."

"Quite," he agreed. His smile edged right to her heart. "Saint Nick might even recruit you."

"In your dreams," she told him.

"Every night," she thought he uttered under his breath, but then decided she had to be mistaken when he added, "Right. You might make somebody laugh if they saw you as Irma, and that would be a crime, right?"

Sharon thought about how silly she looked in her Irma disguise, and how good it felt to laugh, and how happy those children had seemed when they'd been laughing at Mr. Peabody at the center.

"Maybe it wouldn't be such a crime," she agreed finally, and was rewarded by his smile.

"Well, don't worry about my clothes," he said. "Where I was already headed, everyone knows me quite well. They won't mind the outfit."

"The hotel where the Extravaganza is held?"

He shook his head. *"Mama Mia's."*

She supposed it was some small Italian restaurant on some corner in Springfield, which wasn't that far away. "Sounds fine. I love Italian."

He put the pickup in gear and eased out into traffic. Retrieving her notebook and a pen from her purse, Sharon asked, "Now, about this press conference today—I thought Saint Nick shunned publicity. So what was the thing at the shelter about?"

"Don't you ever forget about your job?"

"Don't you ever take life seriously?"

Stopping at a light, Nick scanned her critically, his smile gone. For one or two seconds earlier, she'd seemed to be softening. His mistake. "What do you think I was doing there?"

"I don't want to speculate."

"A reporter doesn't want to speculate? Hell, lady, you've already thought it through and made your decision, and you're just waiting for me to verify it. So why don't you tell me what you're thinking about Saint Nick's press conference and clear the air." He took an entrance onto Interstate 44.

"I believe, with only a week and a half until Christmas, that you've decided it's time to make your big push into publicity. Clever timing."

"This couldn't be as simple as 'I read your article about the homeless family and was so inspired and moved by your writing I knew I had to help'?"

Was he teasing her? His face was so closed, she couldn't tell for sure. "I think you give me too much credit."

"You're a good writer, Sharon. You bring out emotions in people." He had certainly been driven to anger when he'd read her editorial, and to help when he'd read her article about Clement House. "You should believe in yourself more."

She shook her head doubtfully and went back to writing her notes.

He'd tried. Holding back a sigh, Nick exited the interstate, made a couple turns, and drove down a backroad cutting through some woods. He was beginning to doubt he would ever get through to her.

"Strange area for a restaurant," Sharon commented.

He didn't answer as he pulled onto a long private drive leading up to a medium-size private home nestled in the middle of the towering trees.

"This is Mama Mia's?" she asked, slightly disoriented.

"It means 'my mother's,'" Nick said, parking. "In Italian."

Whoa! Flabbergasted, Sharon didn't know what to say. Why had he brought her to meet his family?

Don't speculate, she told herself firmly. *Stay in control. Think of this as an opportunity to find out more about Saint Nick and what made him the man he is today.* If she presumed his bringing her here meant anything else, she might only be letting herself in for heartbreak.

"You said we were going to a restaurant," she said chidingly.

"I said we'd go someplace to eat where everybody knew me," Nick said, his mood buoyant again.

"Everyone does know me here, and I was invited to lunch. My sisters are coming, along with their kids. Mom makes plenty. She won't mind fattening you up a bit." Getting out of the truck, he glanced inside at her. "You coming in or not?"

"Of course." She shoved her notebook into her purse and pushed the door open. "What do you mean, fatten me up? I'm not that skinny."

"Mom will think you are." He grinned again, most exasperatingly. His steps crunched on the gravel in the driveway, and she ran to catch up.

"Actually, Nick, I'm pleased you brought me here. It's the perfect opportunity for me to learn more about what made you into a saint."

He threw up his hands. "For one hour, Sharon, make a vow to yourself that you aren't going to think like a reporter, or a cynic, or anything. Promise me that you'll just sit back and enjoy this visit?"

"I don't know if I know how," she admitted finally, with a shrug of her delicate shoulders.

"Ah, Sharon." Reaching out, Nick caught her up in his arms, surrounding her with the warmth and strength he knew only he cared enough to give her. He hugged her to him, and that was all he did, even though he wanted desperately to kiss her—among other things. But a kiss was something different from what he was trying to give to her. Right now, she needed more than lustful kisses.

She needed love. The kind of love he hoped she would feel here, among his mother and sisters.

"Oh, my gosh," a female voice said from behind them. "Son, if it's this serious, tell me she's Italian."

Pulling away from Nick so quickly she almost fell, Sharon glanced guiltily, shyly, at the slightly chubby, black-haired woman at the front door of the house. Nick's mother.

"Don't worry, Sharon," Nick said, taking her hand. "She's only teasing."

"Don't put words in my mouth, Nickolo," the woman said, throwing him a stern look. "Are you Italian?" she asked Sharon directly.

"Black Irish," Sharon told her. "But I was raised Catholic."

Her smile was a carbon copy of Nick's. "That's close enough."

Once she relaxed, Sharon did enjoy herself immensely. His family had a certain charm, especially his mother, whose jokes were a trifle risqué. Through all the joking, or maybe despite of it, one thing had come through clearly—Nick's mother and sisters had put him on a pedestal. Their admiration of him and what he was doing in Wheaton had come through loud and clear. So did their love for each other.

In the next few days following their lunch, Nick seemed determined to make up for lost time with her. First, he'd dragged her into a toy shop, where she'd helped him pick out dolls and other toys his young nieces had asked for that he couldn't get from his factory. Twice, she'd pulled him away from the video game display and set him back on track, but the whole time, he'd kept her laughing. And when they'd reached her front door that evening, he'd presented her with a small teddy bear wearing a red Santa Claus stocking cap.

"Someone to cuddle," he'd told her, "when I'm not around." Winking, he dashed off toward the stairwell. By the time she'd recovered and called a thank-you down the stairs, all that came back was a reverberating, "Merry Christmas!"

On her way out the door to work the next morning, she'd caught herself absently touching the teddy bear for luck. Shaking her head at her silliness, she'd arrived at work to find an invitation to a tour of Bonacotti Industries and a late dinner—grungy clothes required.

Even that was fun, in a Mr. Peabody sort of way, sitting at a cafeteria table with take-out ordered in. He introduced Sharon as Irma to a couple of his employees, but stopped that as soon as she threatened to call him Peabody. He fascinated her with the workings of his factory, and the small, moveable parts they produced that somehow ended up making little wooden cars, trucks, and windmills.

By the end of four days, Sharon realized suddenly she hadn't thought of her mother's death once, despite the fact that Nick lived and breathed Christmas. It was like she was on a merry-go-round ride when she was with him, so caught up by the rushing joy of the spin that she didn't have time to think. When she finally did mull over the memory of her mother, it wasn't the agonizing pain she'd felt before. The change was due to one person—Nick Bonacotti.

8

⟵⟶

Their first real date came three days before Christmas at the Cross Winds Restaurant. Seated at a cozy corner table, having just finished with dinner, Sharon settled back in her chair and stared out the huge picture windows at the lake the restaurant was named after. The Cross Winds had lit the lake with strategically placed lights, and she had never seen anything more beautiful. With Nick as her companion, this date was like a Christmas fairy tale, with her as the Christmas princess and Nick as the knight.

Christmas princess? Nick as a knight? She should have turned him down, Sharon thought. She was beginning to lose her sense of reality whenever she was around Nick. It wasn't good. The fall would be too far when the relationship ended.

Tonight, Nick was in a black suit that set off the darkness of his hair and the blue of his eyes, which had kept glancing at her all through dinner. Admiring, courtly, he was the perfect prince.

"Looks like we're getting company," Nick said suddenly. "Do you know that man?"

She followed his gaze. Harley Gibson was headed straight toward her.

"Oh, my gosh," she whispered, leaning close to Nick. "It's my editor. I didn't know he made enough to eat here."

Nick sputtered and chuckled until she elbowed him in the ribs and said, "You're the straight man this evening. He knows I'm after Saint Nick. Who do I tell him you are?"

"Nick Bon—" He stopped, realizing the problem. No sense in throwing suspicion straight onto him. He leaned low and whispered into the pink shell of her ear. "Okay, make up a name."

Blankly, she stared at him. But then Harley had reached them and was saying hello and looking expectantly at her, so she had to say something.

"Harley, how are you? This is Anthony."

Nick sputtered again, but recovered and nodded at the man. "Merry Christmas."

Harley gazed suspiciously from her to Nick and back again. "You still working on that story I gave you?" he asked her.

"Of course, Harley." She smiled at him. "I'm just relaxing for an evening."

"You? Relaxing?"

"Yes, Harley, I am," she said softly, sharing a smile with Nick. His eyes reflected the glow of the candles, and she kept her gaze on him, forgetting all about Harley for a long minute until the editor cleared his throat.

"Yes. Well. Just keep in mind I want your article on my desk by Friday. For the Christmas edition."

Tearing her gaze reluctantly from Nick, she met Harley's stare. "I understand."

"Nice meeting you...Anthony," Harley said, then turned and walked toward the front of the building.

"That article he mentioned—it wouldn't happen to be the one you wanted to do on me, would it?" Nick asked.

She nodded. He lifted his glass of white wine to his lips, sipped, and replaced it.

"What are you going to write?" It was the moment of truth, Nick thought, searching her face for any signs of doubt about him. He knew she seemed more easygoing lately, more likeable, but that didn't necessarily mean the article was off and Saint Nick was safe.

She hesitated. "I've got to give Harley something. But I'm no longer kidding myself that it will be the article he wants." Her clear green eyes met his, her gaze hitting him in the gut with a jolt. He'd wanted her, he realized. He wanted her from the very first second he'd seen her and that was part of the reason he'd hung on to her so hard. The other part of why he didn't know.

"I staked my whole career on you being just like every other person I've ever met in the business world—wanting to make a buck and putting your own needs first," she said. "But you're different than all the others. You're special. You're—" She paused, her fingertips grabbing for the right word.

"You're a saint," she said finally.

"I'm not, really," Nick protested. She had his attention now. "I've got my flaws."

She shook her head. "No. You're different. Anyway, I got this thing started and convinced Harley to take a chance on me. If I don't follow up the story on Saint Nick with something juicy, Harley is going to be furious."

"I'm not a saint, Sharon," Nick said again.

"You are." Her eyes shone as she refused to believe him. "That was a wonderful thing you did, getting that family from Clement House their own place in time for Christmas."

"It's only money, Sharon. Giving it away doesn't qualify me for sainthood."

Nick sensed she wasn't listening. She was watching him with a tender look deep in her green eyes. "I'm glad I've gotten to know you," she said, her voice as melodious and sweet as the soft music being piped in around them.

"Same here." He was. When she wasn't struggling so hard to keep up her defenses, Sharon could be sweet and caring. She also saw the world with a cynically funny slant he found refreshing. There was a lot to like about her, and Nick didn't want her to lose her job.

"But, Sharon, how are you going to keep your editor happy?"

Sharon had no idea. But she understood Nick now and believed in him. A small part of her had always wanted to think Saint Nick was for real, so it hadn't taken much. A week of Nick's showing he cared about her. Being close to him, feeling the electricity between them intensify until she was certain it was going to culminate in white lightning. She wanted him, she realized. Whatever else happened, she wanted one magical night of being in the arms of the man of her dreams. One night of being swept away to a place where love really happened, and people really cared about each other forever. She needed that much to keep going when Nick finally realized his secret was safe and he no longer had to stay around her.

"I don't know how I'm going to keep my job," she said. "Except it won't be by ruining Saint Nick. Are you ready to go?"

By the time they reached her apartment, Sharon was sure of what she wanted, but now, faced with asking Nick for it, she had the first shy moment she could remember having in a long time. "You want to come inside?" she asked softly.

"Do you want me to?"

She nodded, and Nick leaned down and covered her mouth in a soul-embracing kiss.

Inside Sharon dead-bolted her apartment door and slipped off her satin pumps. Nick loosened his tie, and she unknotted it and pulled it slowly down off his neck. Like the one they'd shared on the elevator coming up, their lips met in another sultry kiss, slow and hot and full of promise as they pressed their bodies together.

Falling for Nick was something she could not allow herself to do, but as her white silk dress puddled on the floor at her feet, Sharon knew it was going to take all her strength not to.

On tiptoes, her arms wrapped around his neck, she kissed him. Seconds later, still connected by a kiss, they both stripped off their remaining clothes as they inched their way to the bedroom, heedless of the trail they left at their feet. A minute later arms and legs tangled together as they clung to each other, they fell backward onto the mattress, and somehow, being off balance felt so right.

His heated skin felt so good, so right, against hers as they explored each other with thirsty abandonment. He was making love to her as though she were special, a piece of art to be cherished.

When his hands slid downward over her hips and his thumbs over the flat expanse of her stomach, she stopped all conscious thinking and gave herself to him as he entered her. Together, they moved with a passion so overwhelming it was Christmas magical.

Even though Sharon knew what she'd just shared with Nick wasn't love, she also knew it *was* a warm, glowing illusion of love she could put into a mental Christmas package tied with gold ribbon, a memory she could unwrap any time she got lonely in the Christmases to come. No matter how much she might want the real thing, this "love" would have to be enough. Unless . . . unless she was wrong and tonight had meant something to Nick . . .

"Sharon?"

Nick's voice was throaty, passion-filled. He nuzzled her neck again and flicked his tongue against the hollow of her collarbone. She almost forgot to ask what he wanted.

"Hmm?"

"We have to talk."

Her eyes fluttered open. She was warm and relaxed, and all "we have to talk" predicted was tension and problems. His serious look did nothing to reassure her. "Men never talk after sex."

"You know this from experience?" He pulled himself up until he was sitting against the pillows, the blanket just about covering everything that was interesting to look at. She danced her fingers downward to the edge of the sheet, but he grabbed her hand. "Do you?"

She propped herself up on one elbow and stared sternly back at him. "It is the nature of men not to talk about anything after sex. If they do, it's because some woman has trained them after years of hard work."

"You know this from experience?" he asked again, the cockeyed grin never leaving his face. She grinned, too.

"I saw it on television."

"Aha!" he said, patting her hand and letting it loose. "You'd better be careful. Television can lead you to all kinds of warped conclusions about people."

"Such as?"

"Such as everyone has ulterior motives for what they do."

"Neatly done, Nick. Is there anything you don't do perfectly?" Her words were light, but her heart was sinking. He was going to ask her about the story; she would tell him everything was going to be fine for him; and then he was going to walk away.

"I'm not perfect, Sharon, and I'm no saint," he said, the smile leaving his face.

"Yes, you are," she said.

He shook his head. "I'm just a human being, with all the flaws any man has."

"Name one." She couldn't think of any.

"I give away money, right?"

"You give away love," she corrected, pleased that she'd learned the lesson he and the Reverend Dunlevy had been trying to teach her. She began to twirl a finger in the dark hair on his chest, moving it downward slowly, tantalizingly, downward. She wanted to make the most of this illusion while she could.

"No." He caught her roving finger as it touched his pelvic bone, and she looked up at him in surprise. "No," he said again. "I give away money. And I know you've wondered why."

Sharon held the blankets against her breasts and sat up against the pillows, sensing what he was about to tell her was very important to him. She listened as he told her about his father's dying in combat and leaving behind a bewildered boy whom everyone encouraged to act like a "man" and take care of his sisters and mother. He told her about his sisters' wishes that had gone unfulfilled and about his sense of powerlessness over life.

"That stuck with me. I help people not for them, but for *me*. I need to feel in control, like I have some power over the way things are around me. My motives are selfish. I don't want to be that ten-year-old watching his sisters wishing for something that can't be ever again."

Sharon brushed a tear from her eye. What they'd both been through in life was so unfair. To think she'd once thought Nick's childhood had been idyllic.

Nick's bare, broad shoulders rose and fell in a shrug. "So first, I got involved in community service.

But between fund-raising and all that in addition to the factory, all I seemed to do was work and worry. I'd been doing that since Dad died and suddenly, a few years ago, I decided it was time to have some fun for a change. I got tired of the spreadsheet and blueprint image.''

''So how did you come up with the Saint Nick and Mr. Peabody idea?''

''When I told my sister I wanted to have a little fun while I helped people, she reminded me of when I was twelve and dressed up as Santa for them one Christmas.''

Sharon smiled at the image in her mind.

''She suggested I give parties for kids in homes and the like and come in a Santa suit. When I told her I doubted I could fool any kid that way, she got flabbergasted, threw her hands up in the air, and suggested I go disguised as the pencil-toting nerd I'd become.'' He grinned from ear to ear. ''Hide in plain sight, don't they say?''

''And no one ever recognizes you?''

He shrugged. ''The real Nick Bonacotti isn't exactly a household word.'' He glanced sideways at her. ''And I don't want to be either, so don't get any fresh ideas.''

A twinkle in her eyes, she ran her hand up the thick slope of his shoulder. ''I've already got loads of ideas, and they're all fresh. Want to hear one?''

''Sure,'' he said, leaning sideways and brushing his lips across the top of her head, breathing in the apple blossom scent of her hair. After years of not having a woman appeal to him on the special level he longed for, he'd found Sharon. But he was afraid. Until she'd called him perfect, he had almost believed the woman nestled in his arms liked Nick Bonacotti, the person, and not Saint Nick, the legend. But what if he were wrong?

He needed to be liked for who he was for once, not for what he could do for people. If Sharon couldn't do that, he dared not give her his heart.

In the long run, Sharon thought on the day of her deadline, pacing in Harley's office while she waited for him to get off the phone, she wasn't naive enough to believe she was going to hold on to the man of her dreams forever. She wanted Nick too much. She wanted the whole basket of goodies—husband, home, kids and love—and since when did she ever get what she really wanted out of life?

Just like the big scoop about Nick she wanted. Under no circumstances could she sacrifice Nick's happiness to get her break, even if she didn't hang on to him. Which meant it was fortunate she still had one carrot left to dangle in front of her editor's long nose—if he would ever get off the phone.

Harley hung up and cursed under his breath. "You mean to tell me that there was nothing at all motivating Saint Nick except goodness?"

"It would appear so," she said, nodding.

"That's impossible."

What could she say? She shrugged. "Like it or not, it's the truth."

They were interrupted by a knock at Harley's door. One of the reporters had a question. While Sharon waited for the two to finish, she glanced out into the busy newsroom. Despite the fact that it was the day before Christmas, the reporters who weren't out covering news were typing away or on phones. There would be no Christmas party at the *Tribune*, not with Harley as boss. When they were once again alone, it was almost poetic justice that she was able to tell him, "There won't be an article on Saint Nick."

"What about Tracy Rhodes?" he asked.

"That's why I'm here. I'm not stupid, Harley. I read you loud and clear at the Cross Winds the other night. You don't think I would come in here without an alternative scoop for you, do you?"

"I wouldn't know. I figured you might be too busy making goo-goo eyes at your new boyfriend to be worried about your career."

"You're bordering on harassment," she said edgily, knowing if she pushed him too far, she'd be bordering on the unemployment line.

Harley's eyes were glittering gray-blue rocks. "You pushed for this Saint Nick thing, and I let you have it. It's my reputation as an editor on the line. What do you think you can get me on Tracy?"

"I think I can find out where she disappeared to for her father. I don't even want the credit. The paper can shine as far as I'm concerned. Is that good enough?"

While Harley weighed her offer, Sharon closed her eyes. If she could find Tracy and if she could print a sanitized version of the facts behind her disappearance that wouldn't hurt the young woman or Nick, maybe, just maybe, she could save her job and hold on to Nick at the same time. If she couldn't, well, she didn't want to lose Nick, but she'd been alone before, and she could stand it again. But she could *not* be without a job.

"It'll make you look awfully good for not letting this die, Harley," she prodded.

The area around his eyes hardened, and she knew she was in for an ultimatum. "You've got till January 1. I don't have something then to show me your instincts can be trusted, you're working the obits and missing dogs desk."

That, on Harley's part, was professional murder. She was sure Harley would delight in explaining to any future employers just how she reached such a lowly status at the *Tribune*.

"I don't know if one week is enough time. If I have to fly somewhere to verify where she is—"

"The paper won't pay for that!" he almost roared.

She held up her palms. "I wasn't asking. But it may take a while to obtain and verify the information I need."

Harley's eyes were cold steel. "How long?"

"The fifteenth?" she suggested.

It took him a full minute, but Harley finally nodded his agreement. Sharon spun around to leave his office and was halfway out the door when he added commandingly, "But not one day more."

Slowly, Sharon nodded. She wanted her career; she needed it. Though she desperately wished she could believe in happily ever after. Nick had given her no promises for her future, and besides, she'd lived too long to believe in any even if he'd had. Things happened. People moved on, died, fell out of love. She dared not count on anyone for happiness, not even a man as trustworthy as Nick. No matter how much she wished she could.

9

For the tenth time in five minutes, Sharon walked by the exercise bike in her apartment and stopped to glance out her front window, looking for Nick's car on the street below. He'd promised her the perfect Christmas day with his family, but he wasn't aware of the cloud hanging over her with Deadline painted on it in bold, black letters. She was going to have to approach Nick about Tracy, and she didn't want to guess what that might do to her relationship with him.

Even if she sacrificed her career for his happiness, she still wanted to know what had happened to Tracy, and what part Nick had played in her disappearance. If she was fine, why wouldn't Nick just let everyone know where she was, or at least, why she'd left? He would, Sharon decided, unless he really didn't know... or he was hiding something. Since she doubted the first, the second had to be the answer.

Full of nervous energy, she moved away from the window. She didn't want to believe Nick was behind anything shady, but what on earth *had* happened to Tracy? Why wouldn't Nick just tell her? Oh, not where the girl was, but at least what she'd wished for.

Someone knocked. Expecting Nick, she yanked the door open, only to find a deliveryman with a hand truck and a huge box wrapped in white paper and tied with miles of green, silver and red ribbons.

"Miss Fontaine?"

She nodded slowly.

"This is from Nick. Will you sign?"

She scribbled her name on a Receipt Of Goods slip and handed the clipboard back to him. Once the gift was inside and the deliveryman gone, she locked the door and stared at the huge present on the rug.

"Oh, Nick," she said softly, shaking her head. "What have you done now?" Dropping to her knees beside the huge box, taking her time, she pulled the card off the top and opened the envelope. It was an old-fashioned Christmas card, with a painting of Saint Nick on the front.

"'I'm giving you your Christmas wish. Love, Saint Nick.'"

Bewildered, Sharon rose and hurried to her whatnot drawer for a pair of shears. Cutting the ribbon, she yanked off the paper, pulled the top flaps open, and peered inside. All she saw was the white, peanut-shaped, plastic packing material. In the next second, the peanuts shifted.

"Oh!" she cried, jumping backward. She was showered with peanuts as Nick popped up like a jack-in-the-box. Grinning, wearing a tuxedo and a red ribbon tied around his neck, he never looked better to her.

"Merry Christmas!"

Overwhelmed, giggling with surprise, her hands covering her mouth, Sharon at first didn't know what to say. "You're my Christmas wish?"

"The man of your dreams," Nick said, his eyes caressing and holding her. She felt light-headed, like her wits had fled. Was he serious? Or did she just want to believe it so much that she was misreading the look in his eyes?

Stepping out of the box, he shook off the remainder of the peanuts that stuck like snowflakes to his black pant legs.

"I never expected you to fulfill that wish, really, Nick," she said.

"I didn't think I could when you first said it." He shot her an adorable, half-sided grin. "I never thought I'd find anyone willing to tackle the job."

"So you sacrificed yourself," she said.

"I did ask Peabody to be your man, but he refused. He didn't think you were good enough for him."

"Oh, he didn't?" she challenged, catching the twinkle in his eyes.

"No. He wants Irma."

She giggled, and went to sit on the brocade couch. He joined her.

"I thought about jumping out of the box naked, but it's snowing outside," he continued, giving her a leering wiggle of his eyebrows. "The thought of every part of me turning into an icicle wasn't especially appealing."

They both glanced at his lap at the same time, and Sharon held back more laughter. "I don't know. I can do amazing things with a blow-dryer. That might be fun.''

''I'm not touching that,'' he said.

''You wouldn't have to.'' She leaned over and blew hotly on his ear.

Nick fell to the bait and, half turning, pulled her into his arms. His kiss was too short, leaving a burning desire in Sharon for more. Nick brushed his lips across her forehead and wrapped his arms around her. With her head against his chest, she listened to the beating of his heart, sturdy and strong. ''When do we have to leave for your mom's?''

''Noon. Afterward, I was hoping you'd go with me to the shelter. I've volunteered to help serve up Christmas dinner.''

''Well, that doesn't sound too bad—'' She straightened abruptly and studied him. Nick Bonacotti at Clement House, where everyone would know who he was? She didn't think so.

''You *aren't* going as Mr. Peabody?'' she asked, askance.

''Of course I am,'' Nick told her. ''No one knows who Saint Nick really is, and I intend to keep it that way.''

''But it's Christmas!'' Rising, she walked to the refrigerator to pour herself some apple juice. Her idea of the perfect Christmas Nick had promised did not include looking at Peabody for however long it took to help out at Clement House, for however worthy a cause.

''Because it's Christmas is precisely why Peabody is going to help out.'' Nick joined her in her small kitchen. She leaned against the countertop and carefully avoided his eyes. "And you, better than anyone, know why I can't show up as myself."

"So I have to accept that Mr. Peabody is going to be one of your alternate personalities as long as you keep up your Saint Nick routine?"

"Would you like me to give up what I'm doing?"

"I'd like to put Mr. Peabody into that box you arrived in," she said, sipping some apple juice and pouring the rest down the drain. "And ship him to Irma's."

"I am soooo hurt. Yes, I am," Nick said in a whine befitting Peabody at his best.

"Don't get me wrong, Nick. I'm looking forward to your family dinner. But I don't think I'll be going with Mr. Peabody to Clement House," she told him, getting her rose jacket out of her closet. It went perfectly with the soft white sweater and dark green pants she'd put on that morning.

Nick didn't say anything about her decision, but Sharon read disappointment in his eyes and in the downward pull of his mouth. By rejecting being in Peabody's company publicly, Sharon asked herself silently, was Nick believing, somehow, that she was also rejecting him?

Trying to lighten the suddenly tense mood in the room, Sharon raked him from head to toe with a purposely bold stare. "So what does this man-of-my-dreams gig you're doing get me?" she asked. "Are you my slave for a day, or just a handsome escort on my arm?"

His intense, inky blue eyes flickered, and then all tenseness melted from his rugged features. "Whatever you want," he said seductively.

"I just want to have a fun day, for however long it lasts."

"Oh, fuuun. I can do fuuun." Nick pulled her into his arms and traced her heart-shaped mouth with his tongue, as though beckoning her to open her mouth. She did, and his deepened kiss sent pleasure rippling down her body. Dropping her jacket, she swept her hands up his broad shoulders and along the tendons at the back of his neck. His hands encircled her waist and pulled her closer to him. They were molded together again, her heart beating like the feet of a sprinting runner, pounding alongside the rhythm of his own.

His hands slid under her sweater and rested cool against the heat of her skin. Her senses tingled with the scent of him, the closeness of him, and with her need for him.

"Are we having fuuun yet?" Nick whispered, and licked the delicate lobe of her ear.

"I can honestly say—" she gasped in a breath "—I've never quite had a Christmas like this one."

He lowered his mouth and gave her another intoxicating kiss. His hands, which were still on her spine, crept slowly upward to unhook her lacy bra and rub their magic heat all the way around front to her breasts.

He raised her sweater and went down on one knee to lick her nipples. As wave after wave of electric shock ebbed through her body, she let her head fall back and her troubles fall away. Saint Nick had granted her heart's desire and, for today, she was going to pretend everything was perfect, that there were no secrets about Tracy, and no trouble to come when she had to insist Nick tell her what he knew about the missing woman.

"Oh, Nick. I've never met anyone like you before," she uttered.

Standing, Nick scooped her up into his arms, more determined than ever to make this day special for her, to show her how much he really did care about her. Maybe she would start to understand she wasn't alone any longer, and she would quit worrying about her future long enough to really live the present.

Filled with emotion, Sharon knew Nick was pushing aside the hard shell she had so carefully erected around herself since her mother's death. He was the first person she'd allowed to get to her, to really reach her, and she knew she was opening more than her body to him. She was opening herself up for real hurt. But somehow, she couldn't stop herself.

In the bedroom, he put her down on the rose-covered bedspread. He lay down beside her, crushing her body to his as he began nibbling at her earlobe. His fingers rose to push through her hair as he pulled her head close to his for a long kiss, where his tongue touched her own so sweetly. The hunger for him within magnified, and Sharon pressed herself against his hard body, against his strength, as though she could somehow steal his power for the days to come. When the kiss ended, it was only so that they could remove each other's clothes, which got tossed over the side of the bed to land in soft piles on the rug below.

Naked, they slid against each other, building a fire that had never felt so good, so hot, to Sharon. With exquisite urgency, her hands flew over his smooth back. His muscles undulated beneath her fingers, powerful and strong, as he moved up and down against her. Her unsated need for him grew to the point that she opened up to him with all her heart and soul, and when he entered her, she knew, in Nick's arms, that she had finally, definitely, reached the one place she would never find—heaven.

True to his word, Nick made certain the rest of her Christmas was as good as its beginning. At his mother's house, he guarded her from the worst of his family's speculations about why they'd been an hour late showing up, throwing Peabody-type jokes out fast and furious until everyone was laughing. At midafternoon when he was ready to leave for the shelter, he had Sharon and his nieces entranced with playing a new video game he'd picked out. Certain she was enjoying herself, Nick changed into Mr. Peabody.

"You don't mind entertaining her until I get back, do you, Mom?" he asked as Rosemary walked him to his car.

"She's a nice girl. Why would I mind, Nicky?" Before he could answer, she added, "She still is a nice girl, isn't she, Nickolo?"

"Mom."

"Okay, okay. But she doesn't have any family to visit?"

"None."

"That's too bad. She doesn't want to go with you to dish out food? Doesn't she approve? Does she think she's too good for that sort of thing?"

"It isn't that." He shook his head and water sprinkled off his hair. "She just doesn't like the Peabody getup."

"I don't see why. I think you're pretty cute like this, like an overgrown schoolboy." She reached up and squeezed his cheek. "You're doing a good thing down there, Nickolo," she said. "I'm proud of you, the way you reach out to people in need. You've turned into a fine man. You did your father—may he rest in peace—proud."

"Thanks." Nick was certain his mother still had something to say. She had that look, and he wanted to escape.

"But make certain you don't settle for less woman than you are man," she added. "Make sure she loves you for you, and not the good things you do."

Her warning went hand in hand with Sharon telling him he was perfect. His mother had a point. If he no longer had the Saint Nick image in Sharon's mind, would she still want him?

He considered this all the way to Clement House, and he wondered if it mattered to her. Would Sharon have liked him the way he was before? The workaholic, slightly cynical man who liked his office too much?

The Lord willing, he would never have to find out.

* * *

Something was wrong. Nick could feel it from the minute he and Sharon had entered her apartment that evening. She'd been quiet the whole drive home, and that was unlike her.

As he watched, Sharon had hung up her coat, glanced down at the mess of white peanuts on the floor, and stooped to pick them up. In that sweater and her soft wool trousers, her long, dark brown hair in a gleaming swoop over her shoulders, she looked warm and feminine, and he felt the beginning urges of wanting her again. But more importantly than that, he wanted the woman herself, responding and honest with him. Something was between them, blocking that. Hesitating to ask her outright what was bothering her for fear she would clam up, he tried the indirect approach.

"Did you have a nice time today?" he asked.

"I had a wonderful day. Even when you were gone." The smile on her curved lips when she looked up at him was genuine. "Especially while you were gone."

"Whoa!" he said, sitting down to watch her. He knew baiting when he saw it. "Does that mean you had a better time without me?"

"That means I had a little talk with your mother about you. She told me you were a workaholic until you became Mr. Peabody, and that women were few and far between for you." She grinned cockily at him. "Why? Couldn't you get a woman?"

His returned grin split his face. "I'll leave my prior love life strictly to your imagination."

She gave him a mock pout, and then laughed at herself. "At least you don't kiss and tell. But, seriously, your mother gave me amazing insight into your character. She said if you had kept up your pace, you would have been heading toward a heart attack. Is that why you stopped working so hard?"

"I stopped because I wasn't having fun."

She nodded and picked up more peanuts. He knelt to help. Perhaps he'd been mistaken about her being upset about something. He decided to try one last time to make sure. "So are you having fun, at the newspaper?"

Her green eyes widened in surprise. "I love my job," she insisted.

"That wasn't what I asked. I asked, are you having fun?"

She shrugged. "Apart from my dates with you, I can't remember the last time I had fun. I think it's widely overrated for adults. It's not like we can get on a skateboard and be young again. We've experienced almost everything, and the freshness has worn off."

"Hmm." Nick leaned close to her. Her hair smelled like a bunch of flowers in a meadow, and he leaned down to kiss her cheek. She sat back and stared at him, a little off guard. "Tomorrow," he said suddenly.

"Tomorrow, what?"

"Tomorrow, you are going to eat your words."

After he left, Sharon decided to put aside speculating about what Nick's last words had meant. She had one more thing to do to keep this day perfect, something she never would have done before she'd met Nick. Picking up the phone, she dialed the only other person in the world who meant anything to her at all.

"Catherine?"

"Sharon?" Catherine answered, sounding surprised to hear from her. "Is something wrong? Are you all right?"

"Everything's wonderful." She hesitated, and then said to her friend, very softly, "*Merry Christmas,* Catherine."

10

The next day Nick called and asked Sharon to meet him in the parking lot at Bonacotti Industries around noon. Sharon knew she was going to have to talk to him about Tracy. She couldn't bear putting off the inevitable any longer. If Nick was involved in some scheme concerning the girl, she had to know.

Glancing around as she turned into the parking lot, she saw a gleaming green pickup. Nick was bent over something, offering her a rear view of him clad in relatively tight jeans. A really eye-catching view.

"Are you bending over for my benefit, or were you expecting someone else?" she called as she approached.

"Since you're the only one I'm waiting for, it must have been for you," he said, straightening. His grin was so sheepish she looked beyond him to what he was unsuccessfully trying to block from her view.

"Oh, my goodness," she said, breathing out. Behind him was a tricycle. She walked around him to get a better look. A huge tricycle, adult-size, painted red, with a basket on the front and a step on the back.

"You really have reverted back to your childhood. What are you doing with that?"

"The Parker Retirement Home keeps it for the older residents to use for exercise or going down to the store."

"So how did you get it?" she asked, eyeing him bemusedly.

"I told them I knew an old lady who needed to remember how young she really was."

Her eyebrows lifted.

"All right, all right. I offered to buy them a second bike." He patted the black leather seat. "Want to go for a ride?"

Years had passed since she'd ridden any kind of bike, let alone a tricycle that looked like something out of an antique book. She shook her head.

"Why not?"

"It's silly," she told him.

"Naw. It's fun. Try it."

When she still made no move toward mounting the bike, Nick placed one encouraging hand on her shoulder. "Sharon. No one can see us from the road, and no one knows you're here. No one will ever find out you weren't a serious, dedicated reporter for five minutes of your adult life." He pointed toward the tricycle. "Go ahead. Live a little."

He didn't understand, Sharon thought. For such a long time she had been on her own, carefully and consciously plotting every move she made in the best interest of her career. So very conscious of her image, she had planned even the places she went to on the rare date she had, so she'd be seen as a serious journalist who had every qualification to rise to the top of her field. Now, suddenly, Nick was telling her it was okay to be silly, to be a kid again, that nothing was going to happen. She wouldn't lose her job. The roof wouldn't fall in on her carefully built house of cards. She might possibly even recapture the spirit of the kid she had been before her mother had gotten so sick.

Drawing a swift, deep breath, she gave a long look around the lot, half expecting Harley to jump out of hiding and fire her for wasting time.

"Move aside," she said forcefully. "Before I change my mind." Swinging her leg over the seat of the bike, she tested and settled onto the seat.

"Feels good, doesn't it?" Nick asked.

She nodded. "Familiar."

"Go ahead and pedal."

Pushing down, she pressed one foot forward on the pedal, surprised at the physical effort it took to get such a large bike rolling. But a few seconds later the bike was moseying along in the open lot.

"This isn't easy," she called to him.

"Good exercise," he said from behind her. "Build up some speed."

She did. After all, the part of the parking lot not bordered by low fences faced only trees. No one would see her, she assured herself.

The parking lot was wide enough to really pedal. A breeze lifted her hair and she laughed, spontaneously, without thinking. It felt good.

"This is fun!" she called back, turning the bike and pedaling furiously toward him. On purpose.

His eyes grew large as he saw that she wasn't steering away, and he dove for the grass as she whizzed past him, almost clipping his toes with one of the back tires.

"This is great!" she said, glancing behind her. "What are you doing lying on the grass—"

"Watch out for my truck!" he yelled.

She turned and avoided hitting the truck, cranking the wheel hard to the right. The bike catapulted up over the curb and onto the grass, and the momentum pitched her off the bike onto the soft lawn.

Nick launched himself to his feet and to her side. She was lying there, holding her middle, laughing with the exhilaration of it all.

With her jacket so padded, Nick guessed, rightly, she wasn't hurt, so he did what came naturally. He teased.

"You still got all your teeth?" he asked, sinking down next to her.

"You buying a heifer?" she asked between giggles.

"If I had known you were going to turn out to be this much competition for my humor, I never would have asked you on the first date."

"You mean, to the factory?"

"Toy shopping."

Still grinning, she pushed herself up to a sitting position. "That was a date? I thought I was acting as an unpaid consultant."

"Impossible. I'm an expert when it comes to toys. What would I do with a consultant?"

"Well," she drawled, her sparkling green eyes running up and down his body. "I can think of any number of things we could consult on." She straddled his lap, thankful she had donned the only pair of jeans she possessed that morning. Between the spill and the grass stains, her clothes were bound to be a mess.

He splayed his hands open behind him and leaned back. The sudden motion brought her forward until she was lying on top of him.

"Hmm," she said seriously. "This mattress is suddenly lumpy."

"We can fix that." Cradling the back of her head, he neatly rolled her over until he was on top looking down, with most of his weight shifted onto his elbows and knees.

"Nope. Still lumpy. You need a little repair job," she told him, her eyes glittering up at him.

He shifted against her slowly, up and down her body. "Think of it as one of those deep massager mattresses. It feels bad until it feels good."

"Oh, Nick." She sighed. "You are so bad—"

"I'm good. I know. I don't need a consultant in this department, either." Tilting his head until their mouths met, he kissed her, his tongue as seductive as the other torturing parts of him. Sharon delighted in the freedom of kissing Nick out in the open, with the wind blowing and the frothy clouds drifting overhead. She hadn't felt chilly since her exertion on the bike, and now, lying in Nick's strong arms, even less so, what with his body heat permeating the length of her jeans. The very air around her seemed filled with heat, electrified with the force of their mingling desire.

Her body arched into him, her fingers caressed the nape of his neck, as she kissed him back. She felt like they were bonded together forever, their bodies in harmony, hers pure melting butter on a slow, easy fire. She wanted him, wanted him right there and now—

What was she thinking?

"Whoops," she said, stiffening. "This was something I don't think I should have started."

With a slightly exasperated sigh, Nick pushed himself onto the grass on one side of her. As she sat up, Sharon shivered with both the thrill of arousal and the sudden absence of his heat. But she wasn't sorry she stopped him. Should anyone drive up, they were in plain sight. "I'm sorry."

Nick leaned over, ruffled his dark hair, and let out a low, exasperated growl of frustration. "The plant's closed. You want to go inside and play Peabody and Irma?"

"No." Sharon took a deep, slow breath. "But how would you like to play Saint Nick?"

His eyebrows raised in interest. "And you'll be Mrs. Claus? That could be kind of fun." He reached out to grab her close for another kiss, but she deftly avoided him.

"We have to talk."

"Uh-oh. The four words that strike terror in every man's heart when they're uttered by a woman," Nick said, watching her every move.

"I'm serious."

He sighed and met her gaze one-on-one, probing her thoughts and reaching over to pull a twig out of her hair. "I was hoping you wouldn't say that."

"I have a problem, and only you can help me work it out." She anxiously searched his eyes, but they held only encouragement. So she ventured on.

"Since I didn't come up with an exposé on you, Harley is pushing for another story from me to save his backside from the publisher's wrath."

"A story on Tracy Rhodes," he guessed. She confirmed it by the drawn look on her face. "Oh, hell, Sharon. She asked me not to tell where she is, because of family matters, and I can't break my promise."

"It's my career, Nick. I told Harley I would get a story on Tracy, and if I don't, he's going to kill my career with the obit desk."

"You do have a way with words."

"It's the truth. If I regress to obits and lost and found, no paper from here to St. Louis will take my past experience seriously. I'll have to move out of state to have any kind of a journalism career at all. And since I met you, I know I don't want to leave Wheaton." She threw her palms up in the air. "But I also know people are fleeting, too, Nick, just like love is. I learned that when cancer took my mother. My only true security lies in my career, and I won't work obits. I'll move away if I have to."

He stared at her for so long, she couldn't stand it any more. "Say something," she said, her voice breaking with fear. Fear that he wouldn't agree to tell her about Tracy, and fear that he would, but that he'd hate her for asking it of him. And worst of all, fear that he would just tell her to leave. She rubbed her hands over her face tiredly, and gazed back at Nick.

"You're going to have to find another way to save your career, hon. There's no story for you with Tracy Rhodes. I'd guarantee Saint Nick's reputation on it."

Sharon couldn't tell yet if he was angry. He just sounded sad.

"Why did she leave town?"

"She wanted to elope with a man her father didn't approve of, and she was afraid the esteemed tycoon would have used his considerable money and power to stop the wedding. So Saint Nick gave her and her fiancé the wherewithal to split town."

"When was the last time you heard from her?"

"I got a letter when they got married last February. She wrote that she was very happy, and she'd keep in touch."

"But she hasn't. Don't you find that a bit strange?"

"I don't believe I ever gave it another thought." Nick looked taken aback. He stretched his arms out in front of him, flexing muscles under his flannel shirt that made Sharon's heart leap into her throat with the memory of how he looked bare-chested. She wanted to drop her questioning, but the more she probed, the more she wondered if Tracy had found the happiness Saint Nick had promised her.

And the more important it became for her to find out. Was there something to this happily-ever-after thing with a "man of her dreams"? Had Tracy found it?

"Let's go find her, Nick. Prove to me once and for all Saint Nick makes a difference."

Nick stared at the blacktop parking lot, his handsome brow furrowed in thought. While she waited for his answer, she was afraid to move, almost afraid to breathe, lest it bring on his refusal. So she sat, her arms wrapped around herself, waiting for his answer.

Nick's couldn't-care-less position, arms and legs akimbo, didn't reflect the turmoil inside his head as he thought over Sharon's request. She had some inner reason besides her career now for asking this of him. As he glanced over at her, he saw some wish, some question, burning in her green eyes....

He didn't understand it, but he did know one thing. If Sharon didn't care about him, she would have written the article about Saint Nick in the first place, and to hell with what he wanted.

It would be so simple to just say yes, but as Saint Nick, he had promised Tracy total secrecy so she could stay hidden from her father. But he had already broken that by telling Sharon what he knew about the young woman.

Rising, he reached down to grab Sharon's soft hand in his own and pull her to her feet. Face-to-face, all emotions bared, he hoped to read her expressions and tell what she was really feeling. "You really need me to do this for you?"

"Have you ever wanted something more than anything else in the world, Nick?" Sharon asked. "That's how much I want to be a reporter." *That's how much I want to believe in Nick's Christmas magic, and in the man of my dreams.* The last wish overwhelmed her with an intensity she'd hadn't felt since that fateful Christmas, because she'd never again let herself want something so much that she'd be hurt over its lack.

"Being a reporter—why is it so important to you?"

Swallowing, she glanced down at the grass at her feet. "The seed was planted when I heard my mother worked for a while on the old *Tribune* staff when it was still a weekly, years ago, and that's all she talked about. How much she loved the life. How she wished she was a reporter still."

"Why did she quit?"

"She got pregnant with me." Sharon's eyes seemed to knife right through him. "By her editor. Who promptly transferred east when she told him."

"So you wanted to fulfill her dream?"

She shook her head. "I always wanted to write so I guess it was *my* dream. Mom worked as a waitress mostly, till she got sick with cancer. When I was old enough, about sixteen, I went to the *Tribune* on a school field trip, then returned, secretly, to ask around to see if I could find out where my father had transferred to. I met one of the female reporters who had known Mom, way back when. She took me under her wing and taught me the realities of reporting. Encouraged me to pursue my dreams of making something of myself. When I figured out that what I wanted to do was be a reporter, she was my reference into the *Tribune*.''

"How about your father? Did you ever find him?''

"No. Probably never will. Probably shouldn't want to.'' She shrugged as though she didn't care. Only Nick saw how she was biting down on her lower lip until the rosy skin was almost white.

Nick sensed the fright behind her toughness, and he didn't like her being frightened. But what he was feeling was worse—anger, for the first time in years. He'd been living a mellow life for so long, anger felt alien, but it was in him now, anger at the way life had taken away all love from the woman in front of him. To him, life wasn't worth living without love, and apparently, Sharon had been living at least half of hers without it.

No wonder she didn't believe in Christmas.

For the first time Nick realized how hard he had worked for the past few years to be liked by everyone, have everyone around him in harmony. And then along had come Sharon, who'd tilted his nicely balanced world.

She stared at him now, working her lower lip with her teeth. Once again, she was successfully managing to wreak havoc in his life. Then tears welled up again in her lovely eyes.

He threw up his hands in a gesture of defeat. Aw hell, he'd survive. She needed him. He had to come through for her or he'd hate himself. "I'll take you.''

"Are you angry?'' she whispered.

"Resigned." Yanking down the tailgate of his truck, he swung the bike up onto the truck bed with a single lurch of his arms. He wanted her to trust him, damn it, and totally believe in his philosophy of making others happy. He didn't want her harboring any doubts about him, none at all.

After he slammed the tailgate shut, Sharon was still standing there, her arms once again hugging herself against a wind that was now blowing icy cold. So forlorn.

Impulsively, Nick pulled her into his arms, covered her lips with his own, and gave her a kiss that under any other circumstances would have resulted in his taking her home so they could make long, luxurious love. His fingers ran lightly down her spine as he caressed her back, making the heat of the kiss last. He wanted her to feel good and warm in his arms, like she belonged right there where he was and nowhere else. He wanted her to believe it wouldn't matter if she never went back to the *Tribune,* because she had him. Then he squeezed her to him almost bone-crushingly hard, suddenly wishing she would tell him she'd changed her mind, that she didn't care about her job more than she cared about him. That she didn't have to know about Tracy Rhodes. That he really meant something to her besides what he could do for her career.

But she didn't say a word, and he let her go.

"If you want to wait for lunch, I'll go upstairs now and make our travel arrangements," he said quietly.

"I can't promise you I won't write an article about her," Sharon blurted, her voice shaky, "but I won't write anything that will hurt you, Nick."

"I think you're making a promise you can't keep, hon." Nick had a dire feeling he was making a huge mistake in taking her to see Tracy Rhodes. But he was counting on the fact that Sharon, once she saw that Tracy was indeed happy, would have enough heart to leave the young woman alone and not write any articles. He hoped he knew Sharon that well.

"I—I'm not very hungry," Sharon told him. "I think I'll go home and pack."

"I'll call you." Stepping back from her, Nick cast a long look at Sharon's tear-sparkling eyes, turned and headed toward the building and his office.

Stopping at the edge of the parking lot, Sharon glanced into her rearview mirror and saw that he was standing outside the door. Suddenly he slammed one fist into his other, turned and yanked the door open, disappearing inside.

Unable to see to drive, Sharon stayed where she was for a few moments, brushing away another onslaught of tears. The last thing she wanted to do was ruin the serene balance Nick had made for himself and his life. He'd reminded her of those days when her mother had still been healthy, of the days she'd still believed in Santa Claus and Christmas and miracles, and bicycle rides...and laughter.

But Tracy had not kept in touch, and something didn't feel right about that to Sharon. Was Nick fooling himself—and everyone else—by making Saint Nick exist in real life?

And God help her, if she proved he was, what would she do to the man? Would she lose him, too? That's why she was afraid to love Nick, she realized. Her father hadn't stuck around long enough to see her come into the world. Her mother had lasted only eleven years after that. If she loved Nick, would he be the next one out of her life?

With a long look at Bonacotti Industries, she pulled onto the main road. After this thing with Tracy Rhodes was over, and her article was finished, she would know for sure.

11

Sharon and Nick flew to California the next day. He was almost carefree, as though it had been his idea to check on Tracy and he was certain everything would turn out fine. In fact, that morning when he'd picked her up for the trip, he'd given her a breathtaking kiss, as though they were going on vacation. The fact that Nick cared enough to do this for her touched Sharon to the inner part of her heart. He was the man of her dreams, and she couldn't believe her good fortune. She'd done her worst, asked him to prove himself and his character to her, and he hadn't walked away. For the first time, she let herself believe she might have a future with Nick.

As he drove their rental car to Tracy's address in Valencia, she studied his rugged profile and wondered what kind of article she could write about Tracy Rhodes that wouldn't harm him somehow, if only because she'd written it.

She had to stop worrying about it, she reminded herself. She had almost three weeks left until Harley's deadline, and last night, after crying her eyes red and sore, she had vowed to enjoy her time with Nick while it lasted. Nick had changed her that way. Even though she still found it difficult not to, she did realize she shouldn't worry so much about the future. She would see what had happened to Tracy, and then she would write an article. If it wasn't the type of journalism Harley wanted, well, she would deal with that, too. There had to be a way out of this without losing her career, or Nick. There just had to be.

As they drew near to their destination, Nick filled her in on the background of the missing girl, some of which she knew, some of which she didn't. She listened and continued to watch him, stamping the memory of his features firmly into her mind. For later. Just in case.

"Tracy may be a millionaire's daughter, but she was basically penniless herself, working as a secretary in one of her father's companies," Nick said. "She hadn't wanted to go to college, so her father had insisted she start at an entry level so she could learn the ropes from the ground up. When he did that, she said she could support herself, too, and moved out. Or moved down, if you listened to her father speak. She took an apartment in one of the economical sections of Wheaton."

"How did you learn about her?"

"Through my sister. Tracy came for free help to the community services center and poured her heart out. Carol thought she was deserving, so she referred her to me. Before the Extravaganza, I had my sister find out what Tracy wanted as a gift." He glanced at her. For a split second their eyes connected and she was flooded with the warmth of his caring. Good Lord, what she was feeling inside *had* to be real.

"I worked through Carol with every gift recipient until you," he told her. "I was too afraid you'd be able to trace me through her."

"I probably would have," she said, nodding encouragingly, glancing outside the window. They'd reached a neighborhood full of lovely, spacious homes. She glanced down at the street map they'd bought and gave him the next turns. "Go on."

"I already told you Tracy's father had forbidden her to marry this guy, Clifford Carter," Nick said. "He told her if they married, he would do everything in his power to break them up. He could have, Sharon. He could still."

Sharon understood the silent warning. He didn't want Rhodes to locate Tracy. "So you helped the two disappear?" she asked.

"That was her Christmas wish. Tracy was of legal age to marry, so it wasn't a matter of permission. I just paved the way for her happiness with money to get out here. Carter had already made a name for himself in sales, and it wasn't too difficult for him to get a position in Valencia's industrial center."

Nick pulled into a driveway of a modest Tudor home.

"Not too shabby," Sharon observed. Filled with sudden trepidation, she had to force herself to get out of the car and follow Nick up the landscaped sidewalk to the carved-panel front door.

The woman who answered Nick's knock wasn't a maid, but she wasn't young enough to be Tracy, either. Pitifully thin, pale, with blond hair hanging straight over her shoulders, she had an expression that read "bone weary."

"I'm looking for Tracy Carter," Nick said, frowning.

"She doesn't live here anymore." The woman pulled back and almost slammed the door in his face, but Nick blocked the move, shoving his body half over the threshold.

"The name on the mailbox is Carter, and this is her last known address," he said.

Sharon's heart skittered. The forcefulness was so unlike him. Before she could open her mouth to suggest they leave, the blonde reached into the pocket of her flowered skirt and pulled out something she couldn't see until Nick backed up onto the porch in front of her. Tilting her head to one side of his body, she saw, clutched in the woman's shaking hands, a small pistol pointed straight at them.

Sharon stopped breathing. "Uh, Nick, that looks real," Sharon strained to say.

"It is," the woman said flatly. "Get off my property."

"Are you going to shoot me," Nick asked in a lazy voice, "and then call the police? Or will you call the police first and let *them* ask you where Tracy Rhodes is?"

She waved the pistol under his nose.

"Nick, I'm the reporter here," Sharon said over his shoulder. "Maybe I should ask the questions. Like, why don't we leave the lady alone?"

Nick turned his head toward her and winked. To the woman, he said, "If you're going to shoot, get it over with. I hope you have a towel ready."

"This is no time for jokes," Sharon snapped.

Nick chuckled softly and said, "Don't worry so much, Sharon. I'm an expert. It's only a toy gun."

"It's a gun, Nick." What was wrong with him?

"It is a toy gun," the woman admitted, pitching it to the ground. "Not even loaded," she said, as though it made a difference. "It had an orange neon stripe for safety, but my son painted it black so it would look real."

"Sounds like a fun kid," Sharon said, her voice weak with relief. Her knees threatened to buckle under her, and she reached out to touch Nick for reassurance. He slipped his arm around her waist.

"All we need to know is where we can find Tracy," he told the woman, "and we're gone."

Backing up into her foyer, the woman sighed. "She divorced Cliffy. I think she works at Ruben's Restaurant, just east of the Henry Mayo Hospital. Just don't tell anyone I did anything for her. Cliffy finds out, he'll be furious."

Right before she shut the door, Sharon observed a dark bruise on her wrist. It could mean anything, she supposed, but her first guess was that it meant that Samuel Rhodes had been absolutely right about his then prospective son-in-law. Cliffy was probably no good.

Once she and Nick were safely inside their car and heading toward the hospital, which they'd passed on their way, she turned to him.

"How were you so sure that was a toy?"

"I told you, I'm an expert."

"On guns?"

"No. On toys, Miss Shaaaron," he said in his best Peabody voice. But in the next few seconds, his grin faded. "So what did you make of her?" He tossed his head back toward the house.

"That looked like a woman who could use a saint."

Nick didn't contradict her.

About twenty minutes later they found Ruben's Restaurant. A medium-size eatery, it was almost empty at two in the afternoon. One of two waitresses jumped to her feet when Sharon and Nick entered. The other stayed at the table, bent over a mug, her white-blond hair pulled back into a bun and spider-webbed with a black hair net. The young woman was a carbon copy of Cliff Carter's new wife, and Sharon guessed her to be Tracy. Nick verified this by shaking his head at the first waitress and walking straight to the woman at the table.

"Tracy?"

The woman's head flew up almost fearfully. Almost immediately her face closed off in a blank expression. For a long minute she continued to stare at Nick as though she had seen him before but couldn't quite place him.

"I'm Nick Bonacotti, Tracy. Saint Nick."

At the same time her eyes shone with recognition, her face contorted with rage. "Peabody!" she said in an angry breath, lurching to her feet. "It was you, wasn't it? Playing Peabody?"

He nodded. "I came to check on you."

"You're a day late, Saint." Palming her coffee mug, she carried it to the counter, where the other waitress cleared it away wordlessly.

Sharon knew Tracy was nineteen, but she had one of those little girl faces that made her look closer to twelve. Only eyes lined with fatigue that came from experiencing too much, too soon, and a nasty, one-inch scar on her chin marred what otherwise would have been fresh-faced perfection. The weary look was what made her seem so much like Cliffy's new wife, Sharon realized suddenly.

"Look, Tracy, I'd like to talk to you." Nick glanced around the diner at the several small tables, the fan circling lazily overhead, and the red Coke lampshades. Through a large serving window, he spotted an older woman wearing a cook's apron, and the other waitress. They were talking together in the rear of the kitchen, watching the scene in the diner unfold. "Could we sit down?"

"I've got work to do," Tracy said, rounding the counter to a sink and rinsing out a rag with steaming hot water.

"If you need help, I'd like to—"

"Help?" Tracy's blue-eyed gaze cut Nick to shreds. "No, thanks, Saint Nick. The last thing I need is more of your kind of help. Dad was right about Cliff. The first time he beat me up, I lit out of that house, got my divorce, and didn't look back. If it wasn't for you, I'd still be in Wheaton, happy, with a father that wasn't angry at me. I'd have a real future." Her voice was low enough that she wasn't causing a scene, but still, Tracy shot a nervous look back toward her employer. "I would be in Wheaton learning my own lessons instead of drowning out here in California sunshine and dishwater."

Nick's expression darkened, and a bleak tightening of his lips reflected his pain. Sharon protectively reached out to touch his tensed shoulder, wanting to spare him what she had thrown him into. Making him come to California had been the stupidest mistake of her life.

"Maybe we should leave," she said softly.

Nick's look suggested that she had asked for this, and she was going to have to see it through. Looking back at Tracy, his eyes turned compassionate. "Let me buy you a plane ticket home."

"No!" Tracy practically shouted. "No. Don't you get it? I don't want your help. I don't want anyone to interfere with my life, ever again."

"Tracy?" The older woman leaned over the countertop separating the diner from the kitchen, her lined face stern. "Should I call the police?"

"No." Tracy wet the dishcloth again and squeezed it out. "My friends are going to leave shortly."

The woman retreated, and Tracy turned to Nick. "Before you go, promise me you won't tell my father where I am. The last thing I need to hear right now is *I told you so.*"

"I promise. Tracy, are you sure I can't do something—"

"Just go!" Tracy urged. "Before Myra fires me and we all get thrown out of here."

Sharon tugged gently on Nick's corduroy jacket. His eyes were full of defeat, and she longed to say something, anything, to make him feel better. But she had no idea what would. *I'm sorry* wouldn't be half good enough.

After a long look at Tracy, who was now scrubbing at the table where she'd been sitting as though her life depended on it being immaculate, Nick left with Sharon.

Sharon argued intermittently with Nick all the way back to Wheaton to no avail, but as he put her overnight bag down in her apartment back in Wheaton, Sharon knew she had to try one more time.

"This wasn't your fault, Nick. You've got to believe that."

"I gave her the money to go. I interfered."

His deceptively mild voice sent a shiver through her. It was almost like he was a different person speaking to her. Not cold, exactly. No, she would describe him as *detached* from the Nick he'd been before California.

She groaned loudly as she plopped down on the couch. "This is all my fault."

Nick frowned down at her. "What? You didn't send Tracy to California. You weren't trying to play God."

"Santa Claus, Nick," Sharon corrected. "You were trying to play Santa Claus. Until I stuck my big cynical nose into your life, you were doing quite well at it, too."

"You were only trying to show me what I should have known on my own."

"But your help came from your heart!" Sharon's eyes widened. "I shouldn't have interfered with your life."

"Exactly the way I feel now. I shouldn't have interfered in anyone's, either."

"You did a lot of people a lot of good!" she protested.

"And one person a grave disservice. Tracy's desperately unhappy." Nick sighed. "I think I need to go home and get some sleep." Leaning down, he feather-brushed his lips across hers. "Lunch tomorrow? At Gifford's?"

Numb, she nodded, unable to come up with any other arguments that might change his perspective. To say she was worried about their relationship was an understatement. In despair, she watched him leave, finally seeing what she couldn't before.

She wouldn't betray him by writing about Tracy. But it was too late, it didn't matter, because her article was no longer the sore point between them. He was hurting over what he thought he'd done, and she couldn't see a way past the fact that she had caused his hurt. With Nick in her life, she ought to be so very happy right now, but all she could feel was an over-whelming pain at what she'd done to him.

Her mind weighed down by her anguish, she went to bed, hoping things would start looking better the next day when Nick called.

They didn't. Nick canceled, saying he had some things he was looking into at the factory. A couple days later they went to a movie, but he was quiet, pre-occupied with his own thoughts. He said goodbye after a kiss at the door, in a hurry, he said, to catch up on some work waiting for him at the office. Sharon, asking herself how long it could last, let him be. When the same thing happened again after another date, Sharon realized something far worse had happened than she could ever have predicted. She still had Nick—but not the same Nick she'd fallen in love with.

Another week passed before he called, asking her to meet him in the Bonacotti Industries' cafeteria for dinner. She agreed to go but, worried that it would be a repeat of their last two dates, she wasn't looking forward to it.

When she entered the cafeteria that evening, she found Nick bent over blueprints at a corner table.

"Is this a working dinner, Nick?" she asked, dropping a bag with deli sandwiches on top of his papers and taking off her jacket.

If he noticed the edge to her voice, he didn't comment. "I'm planning to expand this place," he said over the noise of the other workers relaxing, laughing, and talking as they ate. His hand waved over the blueprints, and he picked one up. "I needed to look these over one more time before the contractor picks them up tomorrow."

"Oh." She sat down on the straight-back chair across from him and pointed at the sandwiches. "Are you hungry—"

They were interrupted by his foreman. Nick spent the next few minutes in conversation with him— something about a day-care center and gym he was going to add onto the factory. Sharon bit her lip and tapped her fingers on the blueprints. When the man finally left them, Nick picked up a pencil and began making notes on some suggestions the man had made. He seemed to have forgotten about having invited her to join him.

"Let's go bowling, Nick," she said suddenly.

"Yeah, sure," he said without missing a beat. "You know, you were right before. I think maybe Bonacotti Inc. should plunge in and go national."

It was everything Sharon had predicted at the beginning about Saint Nick, only it had come about *because* of her. Her blood ran cold.

"Nick Bonacotti, tycoon," she muttered.

He glanced up, the intensity in his blue eyes indicating that he'd heard her. His gaze searched her face. "Say what you want to say, hon."

Before she could stop herself, her frustration poured out in a rush of words. "It figures, Nick, doesn't it? The one time I let my heart take over my head, I find some way to wreck what I had for myself. If I'd just kept my mouth shut about Tracy and let well enough alone, everything would be fine for you now.''

"Everything is fine," Nick said mildly, putting his pencil down. "I've started concentrating on my work again instead of interfering in people's lives. I was this way for a long, long time before I conjured up Saint Nick. I just let myself get overinvolved in the fantasy. This has nothing to do with you."

"It has everything to do with me." He was too damned controlled about what had happened in California, as if it hadn't been important to him. Sharon knew better. She'd seen him glow when he'd been helping people. She saw the lack of warmth and joy in him now, and it hurt so much she could cry, because it was her fault. She'd destroyed the man of her dreams.

He sighed, like the weight of a thousand worlds was on his shoulders—a weight she'd put there. "Don't sweat it, Sharon. You can't change anything back to the way it was."

But maybe she could. "You wanna dance, Mr. Bonacotti?" she asked in Irma's voice, edged with a little desperation. "I think'a I wanna dance." She rose to her feet.

"Sharon, what on earth—" Nick glanced around the cafeteria. Some of his employees were watching with interest as Sharon glided back and forth on the floor, holding one arm in the air and bending the other gracefully as though she had a man holding her close.

"C'mon, Mr. Bonacotti, dance'a with me."

Nick rose to his feet, grabbed her jacket, and rounded the table to take her hand. Within seconds he had spirited her outside through the fire exit, where they stood in the light of the overhead security beacons.

"What in blue blazes were you doing in there?" he asked, slipping her jacket around her shoulders.

The icy cold burning her throat, she took a deep breath and shook her head sadly. "You forgot how to listen to the music, Nick. Saint Nick would have gotten up and danced with me."

"Saint Nick is gone, Sharon," he said harshly. "I gave him a one-way ticket to the North Pole."

"I want him back," she said, grief rippling through her. "Because I think I might be in love with the man you were."

"If that's true, then you aren't in love with me." And that, Nick thought, hurt him worse than anything ever had. As he met Sharon's eyes, his heart sank. He'd taken a chance and hoped for real love with Sharon, thinking that the cynical young woman who asked no one for anything might be the one person in his life who could see beyond his Saint Nick image to the man he was beneath and love him even when he wasn't giving to others. But that hadn't happened.

Now he realized how risky his giveaways really were—not only had he cost Tracy Rhodes her happiness, he'd alienated Sharon, the only woman who presented enough of a challenge to him to make him think he'd never grow bored with her at his side. But they weren't meant to be together. He needed her to accept him unconditionally, not just when he was being a "Saint." She couldn't, and that, like everything else horrible in his life, was that.

Burying his heartbreak in some deep place inside him, Nick clutched her shoulders, impatient. "Look, what happened to Tracy was unpardonable," he said. "I should have realized there was a possibility that Samuel Rhodes might have been right about Cliff. This could have ended in a catastrophe, and it would have been my fault. It was bad enough she got beaten up. What if Cliff had killed her?"

"We've been through this," she insisted stubbornly, her voice rising in the hope that he would finally listen to her. "They would have gotten the money they needed to leave somewhere else if they were determined to go."

"But I gave Tracy more than money," Nick said, his voice self-mocking. "I gave her the courage to leave her father, and the blessing of someone with power. I did a lot of thinking those first couple days back here, and I decided that's all she was really looking for anyway. You were right, after all. The people in Wheaton idolize Saint Nick because they think he's going to solve their problems and take care of them. And if he can't—" He shook his head. "If *I* can't, I have to be prepared to take the blame for what happens afterward. I'm not helping anyone to change—"

"That's not true, Nick. You are. You've made a big difference in my life."

His eyes were crisp with irritation. "No, *you* changed your life. You changed what you wanted to be. Remember that, Sharon."

"Nick—"

"What do you want out of me, anyway?"

"I want what Santa promised me at the Extravaganza, and what you gave me on Christmas day. I want the man of my dreams." She began to shiver despite the warmth of her jacket. "What can I do to get him back?"

"Nothing." Blunt, harsh, Nick's voice was as cold as the air that frosted as they spoke. There was no sense giving her any hope when he no longer had any. "He doesn't exist any longer. You're free to write your article and save your job, Sharon. I won't mind, because you'll be right about what I did." He paused. "And if you change your mind about us—"

She shook her head. "There is no *us* the way you are now, Nick. I've changed, and I don't like the man you've become."

"Then you've only yourself to blame."

As soon as Nick said the words, any remaining hope in Sharon's eyes faded. He wished like hell he could take them back, but if she wouldn't take him as he was, he had no words to put in their place.

He gripped his hands into fists. The last time he'd been this close to crying was the day his mother had told him his father was never coming home.

It was over. Sharon knew that without having to hear the exact words from Nick. Pulling away, she walked back toward the door, her heart shattered.

"Sharon," he called from behind her. "I'm sorry. For what it's worth, it's going to be hell losing you."

Slowly she turned, caught his piercing gaze, and gulped so she wouldn't cry. She'd destroyed their happiness, and she had only herself to blame. Even knowing Nick wouldn't blink an eye if she wrote the exposé Harley wanted wouldn't be enough to sustain her. It only made the pain worse, because the old Nick *would* have cared.

Shaking her head, her composure so fragile she dared not speak, Sharon turned and walked back into the cafeteria for her purse, wondering if she'd be able to return to the empty place her world was before she'd met Saint Nick.

12

Before she was due at work on D day, as Sharon had nicknamed the day of the deadline Harley had given her, she sat at her kitchen table finishing her morning coffee and staring down at the package Catherine had sent.

After Sharon's phone call on Christmas, Catherine had thought she might like back a gift that Sharon had given her many years ago—the Christmas angel her mother had made.

After her mother's death, when Sharon had gone to her first foster home, she'd tried to trash the angel, but her foster mother had rescued it. From then on, the angel had somehow followed Sharon from home to home, left in each foster mother's care. When Sharon had turned eighteen, she'd come across it among her things and decided if it had lasted that long, it must have a life of its own. So she'd wrapped it up and given it to Catherine, thinking at least her friend would get some enjoyment out of it.

How strange it should be back in her hands now, when she needed something akin to divine intervention to figure out what to do about Nick. Sharon had racked her brain for days, but had still been unable to think of any way to help Nick regain the Christmas spirit she'd robbed from him.

The angel was inside a bright red box with tiny Christmas wreaths printed all over it. She removed the lid, revealing layers of crackling tissue paper. Pulling back the paper, she unearthed the treasure within.

The shimmering white fabric her mother had bought in the five-and-dime downtown and painstakingly sewn into an angel's gown was now the palest of yellow, almost the same shade as the fine yellow hair on the angel's head. Some of the sparkles on the gossamer wings had shed onto the angel's skirt. But the face was the same as Sharon remembered from that Christmas when she was eleven—bright blue eyes and a comforting smile—and so was the feeling in Sharon's heart. Nick had taught her how to believe in Christmas again.

"Let Nick be happy," she whispered, stroking the angel's skirt the way she had when she'd prayed for her mother. "If you can't give me the man of my dreams, then help me find a way to undo the wrong I've done to him. He deserves so much for the good he's done."

She closed her eyes. While she hoped for a miracle that would bring Nick and her back together, she would be willing to settle for his being happy if she had to. She meant that with all her heart.

Unwilling to exile the angel once again, Sharon lifted it out of the box, paper and all, and left it in the middle of her table where she could see it when she got home. It gave her hope that maybe someone, some-where, was watching over her and was going to help her out on this one.

Then she went to work. The days since her argu-ment with Nick had been bad—she'd spent them walking vapidly through whatever assignments Har-ley gave her, realizing she no longer cared about them. Without Nick, her life was reduced to an eight-to-five job, because that's all being a reporter was to her now—a job. It wasn't her life. Nick's love, his energy, his emotion, had been her life, and she wanted him back as he was. Not married to his business. She wanted the Nick who met life head-on.

But this was her day of reckoning, and now, as Sharon faced the computer screen to write the article on Saint Nick's involvement with Tracy Rhodes, all she could think about was what she had done to Nick. She had ruined a man who was too good to be true. Really too good to be true. And she didn't know how to fix it.

She could call Nick, but what good would it do? Nothing had changed for him, or he would have come to her, she was certain. Besides, conversation had never been her strong point. Writing had.

She thought about that. There had to be a way she could appeal to Nick through her writing, through her heart. But at the same time she wasn't naive enough to think Harley would accept an article from her that wasn't the full-fledged scoop she'd promised him. If only there was some way she could get a letter to Nick in the paper herself on the front page, where Nick would be certain to see it....

There was. In an eyeblink, she remembered what Catherine had taught her before she'd left the paper, when she'd been Harley's assistant.

Hope surging through her, she tapped out Catherine's number in St. Louis. Ten minutes later she had the information she needed—assuming nothing had changed in the past three years—along with the older woman's blessing.

In five minutes flat Sharon had worked out her full plan. It carried a great deal of risk. If it didn't work, she had no doubt Nick would end up hating her. If it did work, Harley would fire her when he discovered what she'd done. But the only thing that mattered to her now was Nick, and getting back the man she'd destroyed.

Her heart thumping wildly, Sharon began typing out the article Harley wanted.

Nick felt like a tiger with a thorn in his paw, and he knew he'd been acting like one since the night of his fight with Sharon. He wanted to fix her hurt over his changing, but he didn't know how. When reality had hit, he'd lost his spirit, and he couldn't regain that despite the fact that Tracy Rhodes had returned home, reconciled with her father, and phoned him with an apology. Tracy's change of heart didn't mean a thing. He'd been kidding himself, acting like a twelve-year-old, trying to live out the youth that had been robbed from him when his father had died.

You're the man of the house now, Nickolo, his uncles had said to him. *You have to take care of your sisters and your mother.* He'd taken their advice so seriously that he'd ceased to have fun until that first Christmas when he'd played Saint Nick. Doing that had been so much fun that he'd guessed he'd gone overboard after that, looking for ways to make people happy, giving them what they thought they needed.

Tracy Rhodes had shown him he had no business acting like an irresponsible kid by interfering in people's lives. Sure, Tracy was okay now. But what about Sharon? He'd changed her, and now she was rejecting him. The hell of it was, the old Sharon, the cynical workaholic one, probably would have adored him as he was now. No. He'd learned his lesson.

A thousand times since their fight he'd lifted up the phone to call her. But she didn't want him. He had to accept that. She wanted Saint Nick.

The phone on his desk rang. He ran his fingers through his hair, trying to push back the weariness he felt all the time these days, even after a full night's sleep. It was only three-thirty, and already he wished he could go home and go to bed. Hide. That's what he wanted to do.

His secretary buzzed. "The editor of the *Tribune* is on the line."

Nick scowled, remembering the night he'd been introduced to Harley Gibson. The man knew him as Anthony, for Christ's sake. What was going on now? Unless this was something about Sharon—could something have happened to her and she'd left his number?

Panic made him yank up the phone and punch the flashing button. "Nick Bonacotti."

"This is Harley Gibson, *Wheaton Tribune*. First, I have to tell you I'm recording this."

"Yeah." What the hell was going on?

"Tracy Rhodes is back in town. Did you know that?"

This felt like a fishing expedition to Nick. "You made it your headline yesterday. How could I miss it?"

"She verified the fact that you are the Saint Nick of Wheaton. Would you like to offer any comments before we go to press?"

"Go to press on what?"

"On how you almost ruined Tracy's life."

"Hell, no, I don't have any comments," he barked. His heart sank. Sharon had written about him after all. He knew he'd blurted out that she could, but still... "Tracy Rhodes told you I ruined her life?" After her phone call to him, apologizing. Well, his life had finally started falling apart just like everyone elses in the world. If this kept up, pretty soon he'd be a guest on a talk show.

"My reporters do excellent work, *Anthony*. So why don't you just verify what we both know to be true?"

"How did you find out my real name?"

"Since we've already met, Mr. Bonacotti, I'll tell you the truth. My connection at the Cross Winds happened to see your name on your credit card receipt. I followed Sharon to the airport the day you two left for California. It wasn't hard to put two and two together when she handed in her article today saying she'd gone to California with Saint Nick and seen Tracy Rhodes firsthand. Any comment, Mr. Bonacotti?''

''None.'' Nick crashed down the phone, his heart slamming against his ribs. Finding Tracy's home phone number, he tapped it out, identified himself, and waited while a maid went to find her.

''You told the *Tribune* I was Saint Nick?'' he asked when Tracy finally came on the line.

''Was that wrong?'' Her tone had changed from California. It was airy and cheerful now. ''The guy told me the woman who had come with you to California was a reporter on his paper and asked if it was true that you were Saint Nick.''

''What was his name?''

''Some editor. Harley something or other.'' She drew an audible breath. ''Anyway, I assumed if that woman knew and I knew, it wasn't a secret anymore.''

He cursed under his breath.

''Oh, Nick, was I wrong? I'm so sorry—''

''Don't worry about it. Just do me a favor and if anyone calls you at all, ever again, tell them you have no idea who Saint Nick is.''

''Of course. I'm so sorry—''

Saying goodbye, he hung up the phone. Sharon hadn't necessarily given anyone his name, he told himself. All she had done was what he'd told her she could do in a fit of anger—written her exposé.

When that article hit the papers tomorrow, his life was going to be hell. People would line up at his doorstep wanting favors. He was ruined.

Who was he kidding? He'd been ruined the second Sharon had walked out of his life, and it had nothing to do with her article and everything to do with him.

Grinning widely, Sharon walked into the newspaper office the next morning, a copy of the day's *Tribune* tucked under her arm. Despite her fear that something could go wrong before the newspaper was printed, the first part of her plan had worked. She'd managed to erase the exposé and substitute her own special editorial.

She knew what the consequences would be, and sure enough, Harley didn't disappoint her. He was sitting on the edge of her desk when she reached it, waiting for her. Without a word, he rose and tweaked his finger toward his private office, indicating for her to follow him.

Somebody hummed "The Death March" as she walked by, but she kept smiling. Even as Harley closed the door and pointed to the chair in front of his desk, she smiled on, from her heart.

"You're fired."

"I'm not surprised," she said, sitting down.

"Don't bother going to Springfield to work."

She nodded again, the edges of her lips lifting higher.

"Get that smile off your face and tell me how you got the codes to change your story exposing Saint Nick."

"You aren't going to ask why I changed the story?"

"It's pretty damned evident why, in the story you did print. You're stuck on the guy, Saint Nick. Damn it all. That's why I don't like hiring women. You let your heart overrule your brains. All the time."

"Like Catherine Hughes did?"

His face reddened to the color of his hair. "I taught that woman everything I knew. I took you on as a cub reporter to please her. All my energy wasted. She left all that training just to get married and have babies."

"She's happy, Harley. Doesn't that count for something?"

"I could have made her happy," Harley said sullenly.

"She said you were married to this job. She said you told her children were out of the question."

"Goddamn." He assessed her with cold eyes. "She gave you the code, didn't she?"

Sharon stared back at him, her face void of expression.

"Yeah. She did. Damned women. I wouldn't hire any of you if the government didn't have those anti-discrimination laws. At least you gave me a legitimate reason to fire you."

"Is that all, Harley?"

"You can clear out your desk now. I'll have accounting mail you your final check."

She nodded and stood, slapping the paper in her hand. "Harley?"

She could have sworn he growled.

"You should take up a hobby. You're obsessed with this paper. That isn't good for your health."

He picked up a globe paperweight as if to pitch it, and she hotfooted it out of the office.

"One down," she said under her breath. Now, everything depended on Nick.

The day of disaster. Nick glanced outside the front window of his apartment building before he ventured downstairs, and was pleased to see no one lining up in wait to ask Saint Nick for a miracle. Hurrying down to his car, he drove five miles uptown to a supermarket where no one knew Nick Bonacotti, and bought the *Tribune*, which he folded in two until he was in the relative privacy of his car.

Sucking in a deep breath, he spread the paper out over the steering wheel. There, in the lower right-hand corner of the paper was an article entitled Whatever Happened to Saint Nick? written by Sharon. No picture of himself adorned the article, and he thanked God for that, at least.

His big hands trembled a bit as he began to read. To know what had happened was one thing. To see himself condemned in print for all to read was like a public execution.

The article started with a reminder of what Saint Nick did once a year, and a short description of the

Extravaganza. Nick could almost hear her soft voice speaking as he continued to read.

Cynically, I asked Saint Nick for the man of my dreams. To me that meant getting the one man who could give me what my life was lacking, and that was love. Saint Nick came through for me by offering himself. Finding his love meant, to me, finding that person who was my missing piece, that person who could give me what no other could simply by loving me. And just as he has mended the lives of so many others, Saint Nick changed me. Made me remember what fun and joy are. Made me love Christmas again. Changed me forever.

But Saint Nick has left the city of Wheaton, and it was all my fault. I fell in love with the man of my dreams, but I didn't trust him, and, with my cynicism, I changed him into just another ordinary man. I'm writing this article to say I apologize to you, readers, for taking away the spirit of Christmas from your city. But more than that, I'm apologizing to Saint Nick for taking Christmas away from him. He deserved much better than that from me.

Saint Nick, wherever you are right now, please come back. You made the world a better place, and Wheaton needs you. I need you. Desperately.

Nick tossed the paper onto the seat next to him. This wasn't the article Harley had been about to print, he was certain of it, or the editor wouldn't have called him about Tracy Rhodes. Somehow, Sharon had stopped his name from being released.

He picked up his car phone and called the *Tribune,* asking for Harley.

"You know who this is," Nick said. "What happened to the exposé?"

"Your little girlfriend tapped into the computers while I was on break. I fired her. She erased her original and the copies, and put in her own article right after I did the final proof. You lucked out for a day, Bonacotti. But it's a hot story, and I still have the facts—"

"But you no longer have Sharon to back them up," Nick said pleasantly. "You'll also find Tracy to be a very unreliable source in the future. Not only that, I'll sue you from here to Springfield if you libel me."

He hung up the phone. Sharon had been fired and was already gone. She'd sacrificed her job and her security for him.

He had to find her and somehow convince her that he needed her in his life, that he could find a happy medium between Saint Nick and Nick Bonacotti. She would help him—he knew she would. All he had to do was love her the way she loved him.

Sharon was getting a box from the trunk of her car when another car slid in next to hers in the lot. She didn't pay much attention to it; there were always cars arriving and leaving the busy apartment complex. A door opened and slammed shut.

"Shaaaron. I'm baaack."

"Peabody!" The box slipped out of her fingers. Rounding her car, she jumped up into Nick's arms and yanked his glasses off. Drops of water dripped onto her forehead as they kissed, mouth devouring mouth as though their hearts depended on it.

"Oh, Peabody, I missed you," she whispered. Suddenly she realized he was holding her in his arms so high her feet weren't touching the ground. She was walking on air. "I'd thought you were never coming home."

"I had to. I love you." Nick kissed her again. Sharon was beaming at him. This felt so good, so right. "I just took a vacation," he said. "Saint Nick wants to know if you'll marry him."

"In a heartbeat," she said.

"Oh, boy. Can Peabody come, too?" Nick grinned.

She gave him a long glance, full of joy and love and promise for their future. "Only if he gets a new suit."

"Okay." He lifted her into his arms and carried her toward her apartment.

"But he has to stay home for the honeymoon."

"I'll personally guarantee it," Nick said, his whiskey-smooth voice returning. "Three on the honeymoon would be a definite crowd."

"But he won't disappear again?" she asked a little anxiously as he opened the door to her apartment.

"Not entirely," Nick said, nuzzling her neck. "I sort of missed him, too. For better or worse, Peabody—and Saint Nick— are here to stay."

*   *   *   *   *

Sneak Previews of January titles, from *Yours Truly*™:

JUST THE WAY YOU ARE
by Janice Kaiser

It all started with one little white lie to one very gorgeous man. But secretary Britt Kingsley had no idea she'd been fibbing to Mr. Right. And now she's in love—with a man who knows her as three different women!

THE WEDDING DATE
by Christie Ridgway

When Emma's ex-fiancé invites her to his wedding, she tells *everyone* about the new man she's bringing. But she doesn't even know any men! So she hires a date—for a week. But after all the wedding festivities, Emma wants him forever.

Available this month, from *Yours Truly*™:

CHRISTMAS KISSES FOR A DOLLAR
by Laurie Paige

HOLIDAY HUSBAND
by Hayley Gardner

YTCNMD

Silhouette

SPECIAL EDITION ®

™

CELEBRATION 1000

It's our 1000th Special Edition and we're celebrating!

Join us these coming months for some wonderful stories in a special celebration of our 1000th book with some of your favorite authors!

Diana Palmer   **Nora Roberts**
Debbie Macomber   **Christine Flynn**
Phyllis Halldorson   **Lisa Jackson**

Plus miniseries by:

Lindsay McKenna, Marie Ferrarella, Sherryl Woods and Gina Ferris Wilkins.

And many more books by special writers!

And as a special bonus, all Silhouette Special Edition titles published during Celebration 1000! will have _**double**_ Pages & Privileges proofs of purchase!

Silhouette Special Edition...heartwarming stories packed with emotion, just for you! You'll fall in love with our next 1000 special stories!   1000BK-R

Are your lips succulent, impetuous, delicious or racy?

Find out in a very special Valentine's Day promotion—THAT SPECIAL KISS!

Inside four special Harlequin and Silhouette February books are details for THAT SPECIAL KISS! explaining how you can have your lip prints read by a romance expert.

Look for details in the following series books, written by four of Harlequin and Silhouette readers' favorite authors:

Silhouette Intimate Moments #691
Mackenzie's Pleasure by *New York Times* bestselling author Linda Howard

Harlequin Romance #3395
Because of the Baby by Debbie Macomber

Silhouette Desire #979
Megan's Marriage by Annette Broadrick

Harlequin Presents #1793
The One and Only by Carole Mortimer

Fun, romance, four top-selling authors, plus a **FREE** gift! This is a very special Valentine's Day you won't want to miss! Only from Harlequin and Silhouette.

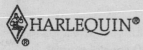

INTRODUCING... **WINNER'S CIRCLE**

A collection of award-winning books by award-winning authors! From Harlequin and Silhouette.

Falling Angel
by Anne Stuart

WINNER OF THE RITA AWARD FOR BEST ROMANCE!

Falling Angel by Anne Stuart is a RITA Award winner, voted Best Romance. A truly wonderful story, *Falling Angel* will transport you into a world of hidden identities, second chances and the magic of falling in love.

"Ms. Stuart's talent shines like the brightest of stars, making it very obvious that her ultimate destiny is to be the next romance author at the top of the best-seller charts."
—*Affaire de Coeur*

A heartwarming story for the holidays. You won't want to miss award-winning *Falling Angel*, available this January wherever Harlequin and Silhouette books are sold.

WESTERN *Lovers*

Available in December

Two more
Western Lovers
ready to rope and tie your heart!

SAGEBRUSH AND SUNSHINE—
Margot Dalton
Ranchin' Dads
Rodeo champion Gran Lyndon hung up his Stetson
to play daddy to pretty Joanna McLean's son. But
was he going to lose any hope of roping in the
feisty filly the boy called Mom?

RETURN TO YESTERDAY—Annette Broadrick
Reunited Hearts
Felicia St. Clair had returned to Texas to search for
her missing brother, but she wasn't about to fall for
cowboy Dane Rineholt after years of working hard
to forget him. But this time, Dane refused to let
Felicia slip away.

HARLEQUIN® Silhouette®

WL1295

New York Times Bestselling Author

PENNY JORDAN

Explore the lives of four women as they overcome a

CRUEL LEGACY

For Philippa, Sally, Elizabeth and Deborah life will
never be the same after the final act of one man. Now
they must stand on their own and reclaim their lives.

As Philippa learns to live without wealth and
social standing, Sally finds herself tempted by a man
who is not her husband. And Elizabeth struggles
between supporting her husband and proclaiming
her independence, while Deborah must choose
between a jealous lover and a ruthless boss.

Don't miss CRUEL LEGACY, available this December
at your favorite retail outlet.

MIRA The brightest star in women's fiction

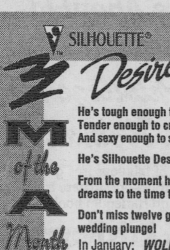

SILHOUETTE®

Desire

MAN of the MONTH 1996

He's tough enough to capture your heart,
Tender enough to cradle a newborn baby
And sexy enough to satisfy your wildest fantasies....

He's Silhouette Desire's MAN OF THE MONTH!

From the moment he meets the woman of his
dreams to the time the handsome hunk says *I do*...

Don't miss twelve gorgeous guys take the
wedding plunge!

In January: *WOLFE WEDDING*
            by Joan Hohl

In February: *MEGAN'S MARRIAGE*
            by Annette Broadrick

In March: *THE BEAUTY, THE BEAST
            AND THE BABY*
            by Dixie Browning

In April: *SADDLE UP*
            by Mary Lynn Baxter

In May: (Desire's 1000th book!)
            MAN OF ICE
            by Diana Palmer

In June: *THE ACCIDENTAL BODYGUARD*
            by Ann Major

And later this year, watch for steamy stories
from Anne McAllister, Barbara Boswell,
Lass Small and Jennifer Greene!

**MAN OF THE MONTH...ONLY FROM
SILHOUETTE DESIRE**

MOM96JJ

You're About to Become a

Privileged Woman

Reap the rewards of fabulous free gifts and benefits with proofs-of-purchase from Silhouette and Harlequin books

Pages & Privileges™

It's our way of thanking you for buying our books at your favorite retail stores.

✂

```
┌─────────────────────────────┐
│  📖  PROOF OF          YT-PP81 │
│      PURCHASE               │
│  Offer expires October 31, 1996 │
└─────────────────────────────┘
```

Harlequin and Silhouette— the most privileged readers in the world!

For more information about Harlequin and Silhouette's PAGES & PRIVILEGES program call the Pages & Privileges Benefits Desk: 1-503-794-2499

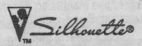

Silhouette®

YT-PP81